AUSTIN and EMILY

a novel by

Frank Turner Hollon

AUSTIN and EMILY

a novel by

Frank Turner Hollon

MacAdam/Cage
155 Sansome Street, Suite 550
San Francisco, CA 94104
www.macadamcage.com

Library of Congress Cataloging-in-Publication Data

Hollon, Frank Turner, 1963-
  Austin & Emily : a novel / by Frank Turner Hollon.
    p. cm.
  ISBN 978-1-59692-373-7
  I. Title. II. Title: Austin and Emily.
  PS3608.O494A95 2009
  813'.6—dc22

                              2009023787

Printed in the United States of America
10 9 8 7 6 5 4 3 2 1

Book and cover design by Dorothy Carico Smith

For the Olympic boys:

Mike, Kip, Kevin, Schroeder, Tim, Cary, and Bobby

When you plant lettuce, if it does not grow well, you don't blame the lettuce. You look into the reasons it is not doing well. It may need fertilizer, or more water, or less sun. You never blame the lettuce. Yet if we have problems with those we love, we blame the other person. But if we know how to take care of them, they will grow well, like lettuce. Blaming has no positive effect at all, nor does trying to persuade using reason and arguments. That is my experience. No blame, no reasoning, no argument, just understanding. If you understand, and you show that you understand, you can love, and the situation will change.

—*Thich Nhat Hanh, Vietnamese Buddhist Monk*

Part One

AUSTIN McADOO

"Faults are beauties in a lover's eye." —*Theocritus*

CHAPTER 1

Emily Dooley was a twenty-three-year-old stripper. She was good at it. Always smiling while she danced, standing up, turning around, bending over and looking between her open legs, her brown hair hanging down, a hand on each ass cheek, dollar bills scattered around her high-heeled shoes. She had become morally ambiguous. Barely able to separate right from wrong, and too busy to try.

"Why would a man want to sit there and just stare at my privates?" she would say. Not just one demented, lonely, nasty man with a glass eye and greasy hair, but seemingly every man. Married men. College boys. Old grandpas with chicken necks. They gathered around the stage drinking overpriced watered-down bourbon and Coke.

All she had to do was pick one out, look in his direction a few extra times, and the stupid bastard would believe he was special. The trick was to pick the guys willing to pay for the attention. The guys who handed out crisp ten and twenty dollar bills instead of balled-up moist one dollar bills tossed on the stage like peanuts to a monkey.

Fat guys were usually good. They didn't get much attention in the real world. They were willing to pay for the things that good-looking guys got for free. Sometimes they would close their eyes during a lap dance and Emily would wonder what they were thinking about. She felt no guilt when she threw away the little pieces of paper with phone numbers scrawled in blue ink. Her dance name was Vanessa. They all called her Vanessa. It was just a name she liked.

Working at the club was more than a job. It was a way of life. A way of life almost everyone there said they hated, but almost no one left. The money was too easy. What could be easier than being paid to be looked at? Just stand up, take off your clothes, wiggle around, and stick the cash in your pocket at three in the morning. The girls talked about saving money and going to college. But almost nobody saved any money, and nobody went to college. They just got drunk for free, danced naked, and rubbed their bare asses into the crotches of strangers. Complete strangers who paid money to simulate intimate acts with other strangers with fake names.

There were always regulars, of course. Men who would ask about the weekly schedule and show up on a particular night for a particular girl. Vanessa would talk to some of these men like real people, but she was very careful not to become friends. A man desperate enough to seek friendship with a stripper is not a man to be trusted, Emily believed.

She kept herself clean and exercised at the gym three times a week. Everything was the same until the day she fell in love with Austin McAdoo.

Austin McAdoo. Three hundred forty-seven pounds. Six feet four, three hundred forty-seven pounds, not an ounce of muscle. His pants were specially made. He wasn't particularly friendly, and was born with a small sense of humor, although he was a huge fan of The Three Stooges.

Austin McAdoo came into the club on a Thursday night. He was a businessman staying at the motel down the avenue, looking for a place to have a drink. He ended up at a local strip joint sitting alone at the bar ordering a milk punch. Austin McAdoo turned his head around to the stage, locked eyes with naked Vanessa, and turned back to his milk punch like nothing had happened. In fact, he sat at the bar for thirty minutes and never turned his head again.

It was a slow night. Vanessa was intrigued by the well-dressed fat man, an obvious target from across the room. She sat down next to him at the bar. Austin McAdoo, with his jet black hair and walnut eyes, turned to Vanessa and said, "Is there a problem, young lady?"

His head was large like a melon. His eyebrows were thick and bushy. He stuck his tongue out slightly into the glass held to his lips, touching the cold ice cubes with his red, meaty cow tongue. Emily was amazed by the massive features.

Softly she said, "No, problem."

Austin McAdoo swivelled his melon head back toward the girl. With his sausage-like fingers he picked up a nickel from the bar. Austin was accustomed to attacking his fellow man in the name of subliminal self-protection.

"Do you see this nickel?"

"Yes," Emily answered.

"I'll give you one hundred dollars to put this nickel in your ass. One hundred dollars. You have to leave it in there for five minutes."

Emily looked at the nickel held between the fat fingers. It looked so small in comparison to the big white thumbnail. She thought about the question.

"Are you some type of giant?" Emily asked. She was naked from the waist up. Her well-formed tan breasts went unnoticed.

"Don't change the subject. Yes or no? Nickel in the ass for five minutes, one hundred dollars. No nickel in the ass for five minutes, no one hundred dollars. Yes or no? Would you like to see the one hundred dollars? Laboratory rats need to see the prize before they gnaw off their own teats."

It was a slow night. Emily could use the one hundred dollars. She pondered the specifics of the question, and then noticed the ears on Austin McAdoo. They were the size of china tea saucers. Much like a regular

ear, except bigger. Emily Dooley felt a lightness. It was
wonderful and odd at the same time. She saw herself
having the children of the enormous man holding the
nickel.

People talk about love at first sight. It's been
written about since the beginning of time. It's very
rare, but it does happen. And when it happens, there
are no boundaries. The rules of gravity no longer
apply. Physics is useless. Vanessa, Emily, whatever the
hell her name was, felt herself pulled into orbit around
Austin McAdoo, the largest man she had ever seen.

Emily said, "If I put that nickel in my ass for one
hundred dollars, then I guess I'm just a whore. But if *I*
give *you* one hundred dollars for that nickel, and then
I put the nickel in my ass anyway, then I guess you're
the whore."

Austin McAdoo followed the words. He squinted
his eyes as if to size up the person in the chair next
to him who he hadn't really noticed before. His eyes
glanced down to her naked breasts and then back up
to the face.

"I guess you're right," he said, and then smiled.
His mouth was the size of a horse's mouth, the teeth
like big ivory chunks. Emily leaned over and kissed
Austin McAdoo on the lips. It was the first time she'd
kissed a man on the lips since Ernie Sullivan in high
school.

It was soft. He was a delicate kisser. They both
kept their eyes open, and Emily reached her hand up
to the big man's cheek, touching his oily skin gently

with her thin fingers like a butterfly. For a moment, they were weightless. He was not himself, and she was ready to leave.

The kiss ended.

Austin McAdoo said, "I was wondering, would you like to leave this place forever?"

"Yes. I would."

"Is there anything here you need to get?"

"No."

"Can you fit everything you own in a suitcase?"

"Maybe two suitcases," she said.

Austin McAdoo began the process of getting off the barstool. He used his arms to lift a portion of his weight from the chair and then pushed back slightly to gain some space in between. His incredible buttocks rose, and then he was standing. Emily caught the stool as it teetered and started to tip over. Austin McAdoo put the nickel in his pocket.

"You can stay with me this evening at the motel. My room has two double beds. You should be quite comfortable. In the morning, we'll be leaving at 7:00 a.m. We can go to your place now to pack."

"O.K.," Emily said.

Austin removed his mammoth jacket from the back of the stool and draped it over Emily's shoulders as she turned around. He retrieved a large overstuffed wallet from his back pocket and left a crisp twenty dollar bill on the bar. The large man turned and stood facing Emily. The bartender looked and then looked back again. It was like an optical illusion.

"What's your name?" Austin asked.

"Emily. Emily Dooley." She smiled. It felt nice to say it out loud.

"What's your name?" Emily asked.

"Austin. Austin McAdoo."

"That's a good name," Emily said.

She put out her hand, and Austin McAdoo covered her hand with his. It was a perfect fit.

CHAPTER 2

They walked out the door into the rainy Tampa, Florida night. No one ran after her and yelled, "Hey, you can't just quit. You can't just walk away." On the other hand, there was no dramatic round of applause. Nobody said, "I'm so happy for you, Vanessa. I'm so happy you got out of this horrible place."

Emily pulled the huge jacket over her head and looked across the parking lot. To the left she spotted a long, white Lincoln Continental parked under the neon flashing sign. The red lights reflected off the hood. She took a step in that direction and then noticed Austin McAdoo moving toward the driver's door of a small, red compact car directly to her right. Emily was not disappointed as she sidestepped the puddles in her silver high-heeled shoes on the way to the passenger door of the little red car. She climbed inside quickly and closed the door.

Austin McAdoo did not hurry. He learned many years ago being in a hurry was not helpful to the process of wedging his girth into the space between the seat and the leather-covered steering wheel. He turned his back to the car, eased his bottom onto the outside edge of the seat, pushed his weight back against the middle console, and began the all-important slow clockwise twist into place. Emily was struck by the memory of seeing her Uncle Hoyt behind the wheel of a go-cart at the traveling fair when she was a child. His beer-belly pressed against the tiny black steering wheel with such pressure Uncle Hoyt was unable to negotiate a sharp turn and rammed against the stacks of car tires around the side of the go-cart track.

Finally, Austin was able to slam the door. His clothes were soaked and water rolled from his shiny black hair. The rain fell hard on the thin metal roof of the car. Emily realized she was bare-chested under Austin's coat, and pulled her arms in front to double-cover herself. She smiled, despite the rain, and looked at Austin McAdoo next to her.

"I only live about a mile away," Emily said, as she pointed north.

Austin started the car on the first turn of the key and said in a voice above the drum of the rain, "Then we shall travel the mile in this inclement weather."

Emily used one hand to hold the jacket closed and the other to reach over and pull the seatbelt across her. Austin hadn't used a seatbelt his entire life and was both morally and physically opposed to the idea. A stale odor of meat lingered inside the car.

"What time is it?" Emily asked. She could see a wide-banded, heavy steel watch on Austin's left wrist. The face of the watch seemed to glow blue, but she could not see the hands.

"I'm afraid I don't know," Austin said as he turned onto the four-lane roadway in the direction Emily had pointed.

"But you're wearing a watch," she giggled.

"Yes, I am, but it's rather complicated. In summary, I don't believe in daylight savings time or geographical time zones. The time is the time. It cannot be manipulated to avoid the inconvenience of dark mornings. It cannot be juggled so people in New York can see the sunrise at the same theoretical moment, three hours later, people in San Francisco can see the sunrise. The time is the time.

"For instance, two plus two equals four. Just because it suits our fancy, we can't vote to make two plus two equal five. We cannot simply decide to change the laws of mathematics."

They passed a bank on the side of the road. The digital clock flashed 11:14.

"Oh, it's 11:14," Emily said.

"Maybe somewhere it's 11:14. We can't be sure."

Emily giggled. "You're funny, Austin McAdoo."

Austin looked over at her and wiped the wetness from his forehead with his porkchop hand.

"Take a right at the light," she pointed.

Austin slowed down and nimbly guided the

steering wheel until the car made the complete turn.

"What kind of job do you have?" Emily asked.

"I'm a traveling salesman. I cover the southeastern territory for the Dixie Deluxe Canned Ham Company." He said it matter-of-factly, slightly boastful, and without shame.

"What do you sell?"

"Canned ham, of course."

Emily thought about it and then said, "I didn't know people still ate meat from a metal can."

"Well, they do. They eat our hams by the thousands. Boneless, jelly-packed, delicious canned hams. And if not for the blistering incompetence of the corporate leadership of the company, every man, woman, and child in America would be eating ham from a can right this moment, as we speak."

"Turn left at the next street. I live in the last apartment on the right, second floor. Do you love your job?"

Austin had never considered such a question. He turned the car left and repeated, "Do I love my job?"

Emily said, "I didn't love my job, so I quit. Maybe you should quit, too."

"It's not so easy," Austin answered.

"Yes, it is. Come upstairs. I want to show you something."

The rain had subsided. Emily hopped out of the car and headed up the outside staircase. Austin pushed the car door open with his arm and started the counter-clockwise rotation to remove himself from the vehicle. Emily stopped and waited, remembering again her Uncle Hoyt as the paramedics turned the green go-cart on its side to free Hoyt from the bent driver's shaft.

At the door to the apartment, Emily whispered to Austin, "I have a roommate. She sleeps a lot. We need to be quiet."

As the door opened, a pungent, invisible cloud of cat stink billowed from the room inside.

Without thinking, Austin said, "Lord, is your roommate deceased?"

Emily, not noticing any smell at all, responded in a whisper, "I don't think so."

Austin stepped inside, cupping his bulbous nose in his hand. Two cats appeared from nowhere. He nearly tripped over the yellow one. Emily took Austin's free hand and led him to the back bedroom. The room was covered in clothes and shoes. The bed was unmade. Austin saw a pair of red panties on the floor next to a chicken bone, a disturbing image.

Emily pulled a small blue suitcase from the closet and laid it on the bed. She looked up at Austin, who was still cupping his hand over his nose, and said, "You can quit your job."

She opened the suitcase to reveal a pile of money. Austin leaned over to look inside. It was all one, five, and ten dollar bills, bound by rubber bands, in loose stacks and rolls.

"It's almost eight thousand dollars. I've been setting it aside. We can drive wherever we want to go, maybe California, maybe Mexico, and you don't have to sell hams, and I don't have to look at men stare at my private parts."

Emily raised her arms, and the jacket opened just enough to reveal her breasts. Austin instinctively looked down and then back up quickly. Emily saw that he peeked and pulled her arms back to her chest. She looked ashamed.

"What's the matter?" Austin asked.

"I'm embarrassed."

"I don't understand. You worked at a strip joint. You stood naked in front of strangers for hours on end," Austin said.

Emily looked up shyly. "You're not a stranger anymore."

Austin considered the situation. "I guess not," he said. "I'll go in the living room while you change clothes."

He closed the door behind him and found himself alone in the living room with the two cats. Before he could gather his bearings, the door to the second bedroom opened. A sleepy-eyed girl with short, messy red hair, in her mid-twenties, walked through the door, looked up at Austin, and said, "Oh my God, who the hell are you?"

Austin didn't answer.

"Are you my dream lover?" she said sarcastically.

"No, I am not your dream lover. My name is Austin McAdoo, and I have come to extricate Emily Dooley from this cesspool of cat urine and animal bones. What is your name?"

The girl scratched her red head. "Cremora."

"Cremora?"

She raised her voice, "Yes, you got a problem with it? You show up in my living room in the middle of the night like Andre the Giant talking about excrement and now you want to give me crap about my name?"

Austin removed his hand from his nose and then swiftly put it back. "I didn't say excrement. I said extricate. And who is Andre the Giant?"

The girl said, "Are you kidding me?"

Austin declared, "This conversation is counterproductive and confusing. Perhaps you should go back to bed."

"Perhaps you should build a fort in my ass and live there," the girl said, cocking her head to the side.

Emily's bedroom door opened, and she walked out into the vibrations of the final sentence of the conversation. She was carrying the little blue suitcase and another huge brown suitcase stuffed full.

"I'm ready," Emily said. "If you'll take the bags, I'll get Ulysses and Glenn."

Austin feared the worst. "Who are Ulysses and Glenn?"

"My cats, of course. I've had them since I moved out on my own. Glenn's a little sassy, but when you get to know him, you'll see what a good boy he is."

Austin looked at Cremora. She smiled a knowing little smile and pointed her right index finger to her pajama-covered rear end. "It smells like ham in here," she said, and squinted her face. Austin was puzzled by the gesture. The cats were at his feet, rubbing their furry heads against his ankles.

"See, they like you," Emily said. She handed her roommate a wad of currency and told her, "This is my share of this month's rent. Me and Austin are driving west, maybe California, or Mexico. You can have everything in the freezer."

"Thanks," Cremora said. "Here we go again. This time I think we've got two popsicles and a frozen cat turd in the freezer. You sure you don't want the cat turd?"

Cremora changed her demeanor ever so slightly. "Call me when you get where you're going."

Austin turned to leave, a suitcase in each hand. His mind centered on the dilemma of packing. He could see in his mind's eye exactly where each of Emily's suitcases would fit, and then his own suitcase would complete the puzzle. The cats he could not comprehend.

In the parking lot, Austin asked Emily, "Is her name really Cremora?"

"Yes."

Austin added, "Like the coffee-creamer product?"

Emily said, "I don't know what you're talking about."

The suitcases didn't fit where Austin envisioned them. He pushed and yanked until the huge brown suitcase gave up. Emily and Austin entered the car, and Glenn began to howl in the backseat, a deep, feline, guttural howl. Emily was oblivious to the sound. If Austin had the ability to whirl around and grasp the cat by the throat, he would have done so. However, Austin McAdoo did not possess such ability, and therefore he started the car for the drive to the motel room.

"I'm not really gonna miss this place. It was never my home. It was just a place I lived. I'll miss Cremora. She slept twenty hours a day. I'm not kidding. Twenty hours. She worked at a doughnut place every morning from six to nine. Then she would come home, eat two cream-filled eclairs, and go back to sleep. We've known each other forever."

Austin said, "I enjoy a good eclair. I think every-body does."

Glenn moaned particularly loud.

"How long will he make such a noise?"

Emily said, "I love motels. I just love 'em. The little shampoos. The peephole in the door."

Austin turned to look at the young woman in the passenger seat of his red compact car. She was alive and beautiful, still wearing his coat, but no longer naked underneath. Life was very different than two hours earlier. Austin wondered if the differences were equal.

They arrived at the motel and got the bags and cats inside room 24 without being spotted. In the light of the room Austin could see Glenn was a wiry little gray cat with beady eyes. Ulysses was yellow and puffy, extremely serene, capable of nodding off in any crisis.

The room was small, a typical motel room, with brown carpet, two beds divided by a nightstand, chest of drawers, TV, and a wooden table with two chairs under a hanging light. Austin's suitcase was already open on one bed. He put Emily's on the other. She went straight to the bathroom.

"I love the little wrapped soaps. You see, they always have one soap for the face, and one for the bath. They're different kinds of soap. It's not the same kind."

Austin politely forced himself to amble across the room and stand next to Emily at the sink. They both looked up into the mirror at the same time. The scene was like a circus snapshot. It was hard to believe they were of the same species. Austin was tired from the stairs and still breathing hard. The air rushed through his nose wheezing slightly.

Emily finally said, "I've never been in a motel room with a man. I know you've probably had lots of girls, but I don't want to know about them."

Austin looked at himself in the mirror. He found no reason to dispel the myth of his manhood. He did, however, for just a brief moment, wonder if he had misunderstood what she said.

"Do you mind if I use the bathroom first?" Emily asked. "It's kind of an emergency, a girl thing, if you know what I mean."

"Actually," Austin answered, "I have very little understanding of the female reproductive system, and I wish to keep it that way."

Emily hurried to her luggage, retrieved a few items,

and closed the bathroom door behind her. Three seconds passed, and Austin heard the lock click. He sat down on the edge of his bed. Glenn, the wiry gray cat, sauntered by pretending to pay no attention to the big man's legs. With no provocation, no forewarning, Glenn attacked the left leg of Austin McAdoo, claws exposed, tiny sharp teeth piercing the fabric of the pant's leg like needles and drawing blood to the pale white calf skin.

"Christ," Austin yelled, and kicked his leg upward with such force the cat flew through the air coming to rest atop the color TV, feet first.

"What was that?" Emily asked from behind the bathroom door.

Austin panicked, regained composure, and said, "Ahh, just the television." He scrambled for the remote control, switched on the TV, and glared at Glenn who hadn't moved since his landing.

Austin whispered, "How'd you like to meet the back of my hand, Glenn?"

He held up his thickset hand for Glenn to see, but the cat showed no fear and looked disgusted by the display. They stayed that way for quite some time, longer than either intended.

Emily appeared, wearing powder blue pajamas. Austin swallowed and pretended he was the kind of man she thought he was. A man who had seen such things so often that powder blue pajamas on a beautiful girl in a motel room had become routine, almost boring. She smelled so good and clean. He glued his eyes to the television, where Glenn's tail hung down in front of the screen twisting like a garden snake.

Emily dove onto the other bed and crawled beneath the sheets.

"It's always so cozy and cold in motel rooms."

Without warning, Austin felt his bowels begin to twitch. Typically, he would have placed his hand at the waistline and massaged deeply to help himself along. However, this was not a typical situation, and Austin McAdoo found himself immersed in the share-a-bathroom-with-a-woman-in-a-small-motel-room universal dilemma. The distance between the bathroom door and Emily's bed was so pitifully short. All sounds would be heard. All smells would drift intact like silent brown aircraft carriers. The spell would be broken. The humanness would be unmercifully exposed.

Austin stood. He removed several items from his suitcase and turned sideways to enter the thin bathroom doorway. There were towels on the floor and some sort of unrecognizable undergarment behind the commode. Austin showered and concentrated with much focus upon halting his bowels. He was well aware it was a temporary fix, but it would allow him time to dissect the dilemma and perhaps discover a solution never contemplated by any man before. It was better than the alternative.

Austin exited the bathroom sideways, touching both sides of the door frame with brief friction. He wore a yellow T-shirt, two sizes too small, and a pair of jumbo black sleeping shorts. The color combination made Emily think of a gigantic honeybee, except without the buzzing sound.

Emily had already turned off the TV. After Austin got into his bed, and secured himself appropriately, Emily reached over with her lotion-smooth hand and switched off the bedside light.

"I love the sound of the air-conditioner so close," she said, "and how dark it is in a motel room. The curtains are thick. No light gets through."

Austin hadn't thought of such things before.

"Just imagine all the places we're gonna go, and all the adventures we'll have together. Have you ever been to Mexico?"

"No, I can't say I have," Austin said. There was still a pressure down below, but it had subsided slightly.

Emily spoke, "I've always wanted to go to California, all my life. I've always wanted to see those stars on the sidewalk on Hollywood Boulevard. You know, with their names, and the gold trim around the star?"

Austin listened. He'd never wanted to see the stars Emily described, but when he was a kid, Austin thought a lot about the Grand Canyon. He was told the Grand Canyon was so vast it dwarfed everything and everyone. As a child, until Austin came to terms with his size, being dwarfed by anything seemed attractive.

"I've always wanted to see the Grand Canyon," he proclaimed.

"Yes," Emily excitedly said, "the Grand Canyon. It's on the way. It's right on the way. And we'll stay in motel rooms, and get a map, and every place we stay we'll get a small souvenir, and if we need to, to save money, I won't eat. I once went two days without one bite of food. Two days."

Austin recalled one of his futile attempts in high school to lose weight. He ate the skin of grapefruits, and only the skin of grapefruits, for forty-eight hours. His mother caught him in the closet with a Baby Ruth, and they wrestled until Austin was able to finally shove the whole bar, wrapper included, into his gaping open mouth.

"Tomorrow, I will quit my job with Dixie Deluxe. Afterwards, I must stop at my mother's home in Birmingham to get a few items before we go see the Grand Canyon."

"O.K.," Emily said.

There was quiet in the dark room. Each lay in their separate beds, staring wide-eyed at the ceiling.

Finally, Emily said softly, "I've been waiting for you all my life."

It was barely audible above the hum of the air-conditioner, but Austin McAdoo heard it. They were in the midst of a sea-change, at the cross of a crossroads, staring blindly in a dark room down the path of faith and what feels right, hitched to the wagon of inertia, as each ascended the hill, made the final push to the crest, and felt the exhilaration of life's free-fall.

Emily was glad she said it. Austin's bowel twitched again, and in the darkness Glenn urinated proudly in Austin McAdoo's spacious right shoe.

CHAPTER 3

At 4:37 a.m. Austin McAdoo awoke with a revelation. "I will go to the lobby bathroom," he thought. "My mind has found a solution for my body," he added.

The big man rose from the squeaky bed as silently as possible. Time was of the essence, so he abandoned the idea of socks and forced his meaty right foot into the wet shoe. There was a cool sensation, followed by a rapid thought process, and Austin chose to blame the rain.

Pressure mounted. He eased the door open, stepped into the breezeway, and before he could close the door he saw Glenn dart for freedom. For a fleeting moment Austin considered the possibility of allowing Glenn to disappear into the night and thereby eliminating the hideous creature from his future, but Austin knew enough of women to recognize the potential disaster. He hurried down the hall after the swift cat.

"Glenn," he whispered, "don't go. Now is not the time."

The cat scurried down the stairs, glancing over his shoulder at the pursuing man. Austin rambled down the stairs, his foot now soaked in urine and his bowels demanding the attention they deserved. The cat made a fatal mistake and veered into a small room with soda machines. Austin entered and closed the door behind.

"Well, my friend, you have made a critical miscalculation. It appears you are trapped."

Glenn found safety behind the ice machine and began to unleash a satanic howl, long and painful, as if he were about to be eaten alive.

One wall away, the night clerk, Sandy Shaddix, heard the noise and stopped eating her yogurt. Sandy was forty-three, heavily medicated, and afraid of nearly everything foreign to her. It was her third night on the late shift, and she reached for her purse to remove the emergency can of mace.

She heard a pounding on the ice machine, and another hair-raising howl, and then a man's voice yelling, "Glenn, so help me God, I will crush every bone in your body."

Sandy reached for the phone to call the police but then remembered her manager's words, "If you call the police again, it better damn well be an emergency or you'll be lookin' for a new job."

Austin McAdoo was face down on the cool cement floor, reaching under the ice machine and trying to grab the leg of the cornered cat. He inched further, and still further, until his shoulder and head were completely under the machine and the tips of his fingers could feel the cat's short fur.

Sandy crept around the counter, mace in hand, and gently opened the glass door. She quietly walked around the corner to the closed door of the vending machine room and listened. Austin grabbed Glenn's hind leg, Glenn bit Austin's index finger, the cat screeched, Austin cried out in pain, and Sandy Shaddix bent down and sprayed mace through the crack under the door.

"I'll call the police," Sandy said loudly.

Austin pulled the cat out of the corner and lifted himself on all fours. His eyes began to water and his breath caught.

"I'll call the police," she said again.

"Please," Austin uttered, "please. I must use the facilities immediately. What poison have you made..." His voice trailed to a cough, and then the sound of spitting.

With Herculean effort, Austin McAdoo got to his feet, the cat clutched at his chest, and through watery eyes located the doorknob and swung the door open. He could see the outline of a woman, only feet away, her arm stretched toward him, a canister of some sort in her hand.

"Who are you?" she yelled.

"I'm Austin McAdoo, ham salesman, room 24, guide me immediately to the facility in your lobby. It's a medical emergency."

Austin stretched out one arm, the other still clutching the petrified feline. Sandy hesitated, studying the gigantic man dressed like a bee. Cautiously, she took his hand in hers and led the man to the lobby. He handed her the cat, closed the bathroom door behind him, and said through the door, "Please take the cat to room 24. Use your secret key. Put him inside, and close the door quietly."

Sandy usually did as she was told, and this occasion was no exception. She quietly opened the door of room 24, let the cat inside, and tried to see what she could see in the darkness. There was a strange smell from inside, but she was unable to identify the odor. When she returned to the lobby, the big man was gulping water from the water fountain.

Sandy said, "Cats are not allowed."

Austin raised up, dizzy and disoriented. "My God, you nearly shut down my central nervous system, and now you reprimand me about a cat. If you speak one word of this incident to another human, I shall sue you with the entire legal department of the Dixie Deluxe Canned Ham Company, bankrupt this motel chain, and have you incarcerated in a maximum security prison. Is the cat in the room?"

Sandy believed what he said. She couldn't lose another job. She couldn't go to prison. Her hands were shaking.

"I'm sorry," she said.

"Is the cat in the room?" Austin repeated.

"Yes. Yes, sir."

"Good," Austin declared. "I shall go back to sleep and hopefully wake up without permanent damage to my internal organs. We will check out timely." And he marched out of the lobby.

Sandy Shaddix was shaken to her core. She waited until the man was gone and sheepishly sat back down in her chair behind the counter. It was a horrifying experience, but not so horrifying as to waste a good yogurt. Sandy finished it off and waited for daylight.

Austin was unable to fall asleep again. His head pounded with poison, and the cat bites on his finger and calf were painful reminders. At six-thirty he could no longer sit still and began to move about the room, increasing his noise level in hopes of waking Emily. She slept soundly and dreamt of turtles. Austin turned on the television, flushed the toilet, and finally opened the heavy curtains.

Emily woke with a smile on her face. She turned to Austin and said, "Good morning."

Austin was struck by how beautiful she was. It was their first day together.

"We've got a long journey today. I'll need to stop by the home office in Pensacola and tender my resignation. If we can make it to Birmingham, we can stay at my mother's the night. I'd rather not, but there are items I must get for our trip."

The car was loaded, and the cats found their places in the rear window. Ulysses was quickly becoming Austin's favorite, for a multitude of reasons. Austin suggested Emily remain in the car as he went inside the motel lobby to check out.

Sandy Shaddix stood across the counter from Austin.

"I shall check out now."

They acted as if they had never met, as though the incident hours earlier with the cat, and the mace, and the emergency bathroom visit involved two other people, far away, which was fine with both of them.

And then Austin McAdoo and Emily Dooley were officially on the road. The drive from Tampa to Pensacola would take seven hours; the drive from Pensacola to Birmingham would be an additional five hours. There's no better way for two strangers to get to know one another than riding together in a small car without a radio for twelve hours. No better way at all.

They passed a McDonald's. Austin began, "I believe the invention of chicken nuggets marked the beginning of the decline of human civilization. Think about it, since that day, the world has steadily declined in every major category."

Emily said, "I like mine with honey mustard."

"Do you find it extraordinary that I would ask you, after meeting only minutes earlier, to pack up and leave with me?"

"Yes," Emily said.

"Do you find it extraordinary that you would accept?"

"Yes," Emily said.

Silence set in. Austin always second-guessed himself. Emily never did. Austin was uncomfortable with long stretches of silence, even his own. Emily honestly didn't notice.

"I shall deliver my resignation announcement directly to the company president, Mr. Lemule. I understand it will cause some temporary chaos, however, under the circumstances, I don't think it's possible for us to delay our journey for the customary two-week notice period. Do you?"

Emily's hands were folded together in her lap. Her skirt was particularly short and red. It was her favorite, and it was no coincidence she wore her favorite outfit on such an important day. Things just seemed to be working out for her.

Emily said, "Well, I don't want you to get in any trouble."

"Trouble," Austin scoffed. "That's nonsense. Lemule won't give me a problem. Do you know what Lemule means in French?"

"What?"

"The mule. Can you believe that? His name is Alvin the mule."

Emily asked, "What does McAdoo mean in French?"

Austin gripped the steering wheel and wondered why he'd never thought of such a thing. Inside Emily's head she put together the names *Emily McAdoo*. The weight of Austin's body caused his overstuffed wallet to wedge uncomfortably between the car seat and his ass cheek, forcing the wallet to actually embed. He shifted slightly to the left and gained relief.

Emily hummed a song. The hum rolled into a few words until Emily was singing softly to herself. She didn't wait for an answer to her last question, and she felt no shame. Austin listened. He watched her from the corner of his eye, afraid if she saw him she might stop. But she didn't see him, and it wouldn't have mattered anyway. They drove along for hours and hours, speaking and not speaking, and Austin began to feel the gravitational pull of destiny take hold, like he was losing control and didn't mind the idea.

"Do you think we could have Chinese for lunch?" Emily asked. "I love Chinese. Everything's so little and cute, mix and match."

Austin had been hungry for quite some time and had managed to remain silent on the issue. He didn't want Emily to think of him as gluttonous, at least not so soon in their courtship. Fifteen minutes earlier, on a lonely stretch of interstate, Austin envisioned a hamburger steak drenched in brown gravy floating on a bed of white rice, with cornbread, and hot peach cobbler.

"Yes, Chinese would be good," he lied. For many, such a lie would be insignificant. But Austin McAdoo had never been one to speak little pleasant lies. Of course, he'd never run away with a beautiful twenty-three-year-old former stripper to travel the country. And he'd never let a cat in his car. And he'd never been sprayed with mace. And he'd never felt like this before, not once, not ever.

They walked into the Chinese restaurant and sat

down. The buffet exploded with culinary delights and brightly colored sauces. Emily decorated her plate with Asian delicacies while Austin focused on more American selections such as crispy chicken wings and vanilla pudding. They laughed and ate until the fortune cookies arrived. Emily Dooley changed her tone.

"This is very important, you know?" she whispered.

Austin leaned in, "What?"

"Our first fortune cookies together, silly."

Austin wasn't sure he understood, but he didn't ask again. He watched Emily gently open the cellophane wrapper and then break the brittle cookie. She stopped and said, "We have to open at the same time."

Austin put down his fork and opened his cookie. He pulled out the small piece of white paper.

"What does it say?" Emily asked.

Austin squinted and read. "A grand and glorious adventure awaits you."

"Oh my God," Emily said, "that's a good one. That's a really good one."

She nervously pulled the white paper from her cookie. She read the words out loud, "You will get new shoes."

They looked at each other. Emily shoved the white paper fortune into her mouth. As she chewed she said, "Eat it. Eat it quick. It won't come true unless you swallow it down."

Austin was puzzled. She was serious. He'd never heard of such a ritual.

"I cannot," Austin uttered.

"You have to," Emily said. "A grand and glorious adventure awaits you. You can't throw it away."

"The edges of the paper will cut my intestines to shreds. I'll be dead long before my grand and glorious adventure begins, internal bleeding, and God knows the damage to my rectum upon expulsion."

"Please," Emily begged, "please eat it. I've eaten thousands of them. Nothing's happened to me. If you don't eat it, and something goes wrong, we'll always wonder."

"This is insane," Austin said.

Emily's face became hard. She hadn't wanted him to see it yet, so soon in their relationship, but when it came, it came. Her voice deepened, and her eyes changed. There was an anger in her gaze Austin thought not possible.

Sternly, Emily said, "Eat it, now."

They stared at one another. Austin felt his hand move slowly toward his mouth and the paper touch his tongue. He chewed, and chewed, and while they stared, Austin forced the wet balled-up white paper fortune down his throat to his waiting gastrointestinal system.

Emily's face changed again, just as rapidly as before, and she smiled a pretty and satisfied smile. She paid the check with one dollar bills, and Austin took a few minutes to consider what he had seen. He feared the possibility of ink poison in his blood and imagined dirty little Chinese fingers cutting the white paper, black dirt under their fingernails, and squeezing each fortune through the cookie cracks.

In the car they closed their doors simultaneously, and Emily leaned up and over to give Austin McAdoo a kiss on his billowing cheek.

"Sorry," she said, and straightened her skirt. Austin diverted his eyes.

"We are off to the headquarters of the Dixie Deluxe Canned Ham Company in Pensacola, Florida, but first, perhaps you should allow Ulysses and Glenn a little walkaround. I sense a hostility from Glenn especially."

The rest of the ride to Pensacola was uneventful. Austin told Emily his theory of airborne sperm as the alternative explanation for the immaculate conception.

"You've seen those magnified images of the sperm with the tails, well now they know some of the tiny sperms have wings, much like the wings on a gnat. They can literally fly miles with a decent tailwind and navigate through undergarment fabrics."

Emily crossed her legs. She'd never known a man so smart. It seemed there was almost nothing he didn't know.

It was late afternoon when they arrived in Pensacola. Austin pulled into the parking lot of the Dixie Deluxe Canned Ham Company, a big gray building that reminded Emily of a factory.

"Perhaps it is best for you to remain in the car. I'll try not to be long. I expect Lemule will attempt to talk me out of leaving, but I will be steadfast and resolute."

"Think about the Grand Canyon," Emily said with a big smile.

"Yes, I will think of the Grand Canyon," Austin repeated as he began the process of removing himself from the car.

Austin made his way up the outside stairs. Behind the desk in the lobby sat Lucy Suarez. She and Austin had exchanged unpleasant words on the telephone on at least three occasions. She watched the gargantuan man lumber up the steps, pull open the glass door, and stand before her. Austin stood silent for a moment, soaking up the cool air-conditioned breeze from the vent above.

"I must see Mr. Lemule."

Lucy didn't answer.

Austin asked, "Do you speak English?"

Lucy was unable to hold her tongue. "Yes, you idiot, I speak English. And no, you can't see Mr. Lemule. He's busy."

Austin countered, "I shall have you fired for that remark."

Lucy shook her head and gritted her teeth.

At that exact moment, Alvin "Buckshot" Lemule, the owner and founder of the Dixie Deluxe Canned Ham Company, turned the corner of Lucy's desk walking from the conference room back to his luxurious office. He was a self-made man, an entrepreneurial cowboy, short in stature, with a bushy gray mustache, snakeskin boots, a brown suit, and two hundred fifty thousand dollars in cash buried in a large glass jar in his backyard under a kumquat tree. Buckshot Lemule heard his name called.

"Mr. Lemule."

He turned to see the large figure of Austin McAdoo, sweat still on his forehead from the trek up the cement steps.

"What can I do you for?" Lemule asked. It was a question he'd been saying to folks for thirty years.

Austin began, "I'm sorry, but I must inform you of my resignation. I am aware of the professional courtesy of granting two weeks notice, however, things have changed rather rapidly, and I am required to travel west immediately. In fact, we are leaving directly from here to travel to Birmingham, and then from Birmingham westward." Austin thought of the Grand Canyon.

Buckshot Lemule squinted up his face as if he were trying to read very small words written on Austin's sweaty forehead.

"Who the hell are you, son?" he asked.

"Sir, I am Austin McAdoo, southeast territory."

They stared at each other a moment, Lucy Suarez watching it all.

Lemule said, "As far as I'm concerned, you've never been employed here. You can take your resignation and shove it up your Yankee ass."

Austin said, "I expected you'd be angry. My mind is made up, so don't bother trying to lure me back. Did you say Yankee?"

Lucy Suarez interrupted with a giggle.

Austin continued, "There is the matter, however, of my final check. Where shall I pick it up?"

Buckshot Lemule shot back with an angry smile, "Where shall you pick it up? Well hell, there it is on the floor at your feet. Bend over and get it, and I'll put this size eight boot up your ass for a bonus."

Austin looked down at his feet. "Mr. Lemule, there's no sense being hostile. Turn over my check or face legal consequences and a federal investigation."

Lemule turned to Lucy Suarez. "Lucy, if this man is still in the building thirty seconds from now," and Lemule looked at his watch, "call the police, Sgt. Russell, and have his fat ass thrown in jail for trespassing."

Buckshot Lemule turned and walked through the lobby, boot heels clicking loudly on the hardwood floors. Lucy Suarez smiled, turned to look at the clock behind her on the wall, and began counting down the seconds. "Thirty, twenty-nine, twenty-eight..."

Austin McAdoo had an idea.

"I shall leave now," he said as Lucy counted. "Perhaps you will receive a visit from a representative of the immigration department."

Lucy spun around, stood, and threw her ink pen end over end at the back of Austin McAdoo striking the glass door loudly.

Austin said, "It's foreigners like you that ruin it for the hard-working families who come to his country through legal means."

Back at the car, Emily waited patiently as she watched her man make his way down the steps and through the parking lot.

"How'd it go?" she asked.

"Quite well," Austin answered. "Much smoother than I thought. Lemule even offered me a bonus. It'll only take a minute."

They rode around the back of the big gray building to the loading dock. Austin spotted Woody and called him over to the car.

"How are you, Woody?"

"Mighty fine."

Austin said, "Boss says I need more samples before I hit the road."

"Sure," Woody said and smiled a snaggletooth yellow smile.

Austin popped the trunk, and Woody brought over a box. He wedged the box in the only available space.

"Might need more than that, Woody. I expect I'll be on the road a few weeks."

Woody brought a second box and put it in the backseat.

"How do, Ma'am?" he said to Emily. "You got some cats here in the back."

"Yes, we're aware, Woody," Austin said. He was anxious to leave the Dixie Deluxe Canned Ham Company before word of his unemployment reached the loading dock.

"Good luck, Mr. McAdoo," Woody said.

"Good luck, Woody," Austin reluctantly added, and drove away.

Emily said, "That was nice of Mr. Lemule to give us so much ham for our trip. Should we call your mother and let her know we're coming to visit?"

"Oh no, that's not a good idea. I pray she will be asleep upon our arrival, and we can avoid her altogether. My mother is a freakish woman, best left undisturbed."

The thought of his mother caused pressure in Austin's abdomen. Then he remembered the swallowed fortune. He felt a sharp pain, non-existent, but sharp nonetheless, as he imagined the razor-thin paper slicing through tissue.

Emily said, "I think Glenn might have an ulcer. He always has such a sour look on his little face."

"Glenn is a flesh eater. I hesitated to tell you earlier, but little Glenn has attacked me."

Emily laughed light and free. The sound filled the car and sailed out the open window into the bright blue sky. Austin was both frustrated and enamored by the lightness. He wished to be taken seriously, yet at the same time, Emily's laugh left him weaker than usual.

She said, "He's just playing with you. It means he likes you. It means he recognizes you as the alpha-male."

Austin cocked his head. He liked being the alpha-male. He didn't care for needle-like cat fangs in his leg flesh, but he liked the alpha-male title. In the rearview mirror Austin caught eyes with his furry nemesis. They stayed that way until Austin was forced to look at the road ahead.

Later, Emily asked, "Are you sad about your job? You seemed to really like selling ham in cans."

"No. It wasn't my favorite."

"What was your favorite job ever?"

"Well, let me think. I've had a variety of careers. I like to think of myself as versatile."

Austin locked himself in thought. "My favorite job?" he said. "It was probably the summer I worked for Coca-Cola, the summer after my second year of community college. I enjoyed the job. They put me in charge of lawn maintenance. I developed a unique hedge arrangement around the executive parking area. It had never been done before to my knowledge. Never."

"Wow, that sounds exciting."

Austin continued, "Yes, exciting it was for a time. It ended on a bad note, however."

"What happened?"

"My supervisor was dull and misguided. We had a disagreement, and the next day I was accused of criminal mischief."

Emily looked surprised. "Criminal mischief?"

"I was not guilty, of course, but unfortunately, the cretin supervisor did not believe my story."

Emily was genuinely interested. "I don't understand."

"Well, the day after our disagreement, a row of

hedges was cut to the ground. They were the very hedges we argued about. Mr. Triola believed I cut them out of spite, but it simply wasn't true. It was early in the morning. I hadn't slept well the night before, tossing and turning over the semantics of our dispute. I was on the riding lawnmower, cutting the south lawn. I guess I dozed off. The next thing I knew I'd plowed through the godforsaken hedges, nearly colliding with the vice-president's maroon BMW. It was purely accidental, I say. How stupid would I be to destroy the very hedges I loved?"

Emily had gotten worked up into a small frenzy. "That Mr. Triola, whatever his name is, sounds dumb to me. He sounds like maybe he was jealous of your ideas."

Austin craned his neck to see her. "That's exactly what I told my mother. She, of course, sided with the Coca-Cola company, and I went back to community college shortly thereafter."

There was quiet, and then Emily began to sing softly again, a different song this time. They drove for hours, the sun setting on the driver's side, the little red car chugging to Birmingham, Alabama. They stopped for gas outside the city. Emily paid with one dollar bills. Austin bought a cold Yoo-Hoo and a bag of bar-b-que pork rinds. They were crunchy. Austin was clearly stalling.

"My mother usually goes to her room about eleven. I thought we'd drive around a few minutes. I'll show you the sights of the city."

"What time is it?" Emily asked.

Austin answered, "As we've discussed, I'm unsure."

Emily suggested, "Why don't we just go to your mom's. I'm really tired, the boys are tired, and I'm nervous about meeting your mother. I want to get it over with."

Austin turned right. Glenn released a pent-up howl appropriate to the mood. Finally they arrived in the driveway of a small white house in a subdivision of small white houses. Austin brought the car to a quiet stop and turned off the lights quickly. He still held hope of a painless entry and exit, sneak in, have a shower, go to sleep, pack a few things, sneak out the next morning. It didn't seem like too much to ask.

"I must warn you," Austin whispered, "my mother has a dog. It's a hideous, dirty white poodle named Lafitte. He is the son of the devil. If a frog has been run over in the road outside the house, he will roll in it with orgasmic exuberance until the stench has attached to his curly fur. I've watched him do it more times than I wish to recall."

Emily laughed softly. "That doesn't mean he's the devil. It means he's marking his territory, that's all. It's normal."

"It's not normal for me," Austin replied. "Stay here. I will scout the entrance."

He crept slowly to the unlighted door. All was quiet. Austin returned to the car, pulled the suitcases out with all his might, and shoved one canned ham under his arm. Emily held the cats.

The door was unlocked. The house was dark. Austin and Emily stood just inside waiting for their eyes to adjust. Out of the darkness came a series of barks in rapid succession, like a machine gun. Glenn flew from Emily's arms and landed on a stack of magazines, tipping the stack and scattering in all directions. Ulysses barely opened an eye.

"Shut up, devil dog," Austin whispered.

The bedroom door swung open, the light came on, and Austin McAdoo's mother stood in her bedroom doorway smoking a cigarette. She wore a cream-white robe reaching down nearly to her bare feet.

"My boy is home," she said in a flat, hoarse voice. "And Lord, what do we have here? A girl? Austin, you better call the police and turn yourself in immediately. Kidnapping is a felony." She turned to Emily and added, "Honey, he didn't mean any harm. He's just confused."

Emily explained, "No, no. We're together. We're travelin' together."

Austin's mother laughed. "Thank you, Jesus. My strange little boy found himself a girlfriend." She raised her arms to the sky.

"Please, Mother," Austin begged. With bags in hands, he took a step forward and slipped on a faded, four-year-old motorcycle magazine. He lost his balance and fell butt first to the floor, still holding the luggage. Lafitte seized the opportunity to mount Austin's leg, humping wildly for all he was worth.

Austin bellowed, "Off of me you disgusting little

Frenchman."

Austin's mother, with smoke rolling from her nose, said, "I believe he missed you."

Austin mustered the strength to roll over on all fours as a prelude to eventually standing. Lafitte altered his position without missing a thrust, front paws firmly holding Austin's trousers.

"Help," Austin said. "Help me."

Emily circled Austin and the luggage and grabbed Lafitte in her free arm. The dog and Ulysses were eye to eye, but both were preoccupied with separate bodily necessities.

Austin finally arrived upright. He straightened his pants.

"Mother, this is Emily. Emily, this is my mother. Please don't ask her anything or she will tell you far more than you wish to know.

"Mother, we shall stay the night, Emily in my bedroom, I on the couch. We will leave in the morning for the Grand Canyon, and perhaps beyond."

Austin's mother studied the situation. She began to laugh for no apparent reason, a genuine enjoyable laugh. Out of nervousness, Emily laughed also. Austin looked back and forth at the two women.

Emily said finally, "Mrs. McAdoo, I was hoping we could spend some time getting to know each other. I'm not sure how I measure up to Austin's old girlfriends, but I think your son's a special person, and I believe we have a future together."

The ash on the mother's cigarette had grown

long. She stared at Emily like the whole thing could be a joke. "Honey," she said, "are you on some type of medication?"

"No, ma'am," Emily answered.

Austin inhaled deeply and sighed. "This distasteful event appears unavoidable. I shall take a long shower."

The mother said, "Don't use the luffa-sponge. I found it yesterday in Lafitte's secret place."

Austin rolled his eyes and left the room.

The two ladies sat and talked amongst the cluttered living room. Glenn was well-hidden. Lafitte and Ulysses smelled each other. As Austin warned, Lila McAdoo kept no secrets. Emily liked her.

Austin entered the living room to hear his mother say, "I've been married six times, honey. That's because I'm a wildcat in the bedroom. That's all they give a damn about anyway. The best way to a man's heart ain't through his stomach, it's through his zipper."

Austin said, "Lord, Mother, no one desires to hear of your sexual dysfunction."

Lila McAdoo countered, "Aren't you the one, on your sixth birthday, who declared you were anti-sexual and promised to marry a tree?"

"A tree?" Emily repeated.

"Yes, my dear," Lila said. "A tree. Not just any tree, but a pretty little cypress in the Toliver's yard."

Austin left the room again.

The two women talked deep into the night. They laughed and bonded, but Lila McAdoo, for the life of her, could not figure why such an attractive young woman would attach to her unusual son. It certainly wasn't for the money.

"He's my only child, and he's been different since the day he was born. He's never moved out. His father worked for the circus. I considered his father's impotence a challenge."

Emily shook her head. Lila lit another cigarette. She was younger than she looked, but not by much. The next morning she got up early to fix breakfast, waffles and grilled onions.

"I don't believe I've ever had this before," Emily said. She sat at the kitchen table with Austin.

"Oh, honey, I just thought of something," Lila spoke. "You said y'all were gonna hike that Grand Canyon, I got some great walkin' shoes. Our feet are about the same size. They're brand spankin' new, never been worn before."

"Oh my God," Emily yelled. "The fortune, Austin, the fortune. Remember? Shoes?"

"How could I forget," he said as he rubbed his impressive belly.

Emily continued, "This is a sign. This is definitely a good sign."

Lafitte pulled himself into the kitchen by his front feet, dragging his ass along the linoleum floor like dogs sometimes do. His back legs were cocked forward, not touching the ground, and his rear end felt the coolness of the floor. All three of the people in the kitchen stopped and watched the dirty white medium-sized poodle.

Austin broke the silence. "Is that a sign?"

"I don't know," Emily answered. "I don't think so."

CHAPTER 4

Austin's mother, cigarette in hand, stood at her front door next to Lafitte and waved goodbye to her son, his pretty girlfriend, two cats, and the little red car full of ham. She started to say something out loud to herself and then stopped. Lila McAdoo smiled and shook her head. For a moment, a tiny moment, she remembered what it was like to be young, and free, with so many places to go, but nowhere to be. She had never thought her son would ever know such a feeling, but now she stood and waved goodbye as he drove off down the street.

It hadn't been particularly easy raising Austin. He was smart and peculiar. His rolls of fat became walls, barriers, and sometimes excuses between himself and the rest of the world. Lila had to give Austin a swift kick in the ass occasionally to move him forward. She knew he needed a strong male influence. Hell, she could have used one herself, but for some reason, or a list of reasons, Lila McAdoo attracted extremely large men prone to long periods of laziness and lack of self-esteem. She promised herself upon the birth of her only child that she would not allow Austin P. McAdoo to become such a man.

She had him awake ready for school every day, rain or shine. When kids made fun of Austin, she had him memorize comeback lines like, "Is that a pimple, or did your face explode?" and "Is that your I.Q. or your shoe size, because your feet don't look that small?"

He didn't want to work at the Coca-Cola company that summer. All his other jobs had been inside in the cool air-conditioning. Lila virtually dragged the huge man-child out of his bed like a whale in the surf. She whipped, cussed, begged, and bribed, and wouldn't you know it, Austin got fired for destroying the fancy hedges around the parking lot. She knew damned well he didn't do it on purpose, mostly because Austin had a roaring bark, followed by no bite at all. Lila ended up giving Mr. Triola a cussin' like he'd probably never heard, but when it was done she was left with the best-case scenario that her son had fallen asleep on a riding lawnmower in the middle of the morning and failed to awaken until he had obliterated a seven-foot hedgerow.

He was a man now, at least legally. Austin was almost thirty years old, and although he never got a place of his own, or stayed with the same employer more than six months, he managed to explore the world outside his room. This was different though. Lila McAdoo felt a twinge of pride in her chest. Her boy was going out for his own grand and glorious adventure. He would have a journey, his own journey, and maybe one day Austin McAdoo would stand in his doorway and wave goodbye to his own child.

Lafitte spotted a large dead toad in the roadway. He shot like a flash to the spot and rolled with enthusiasm in the remains. When finished, Lafitte popped to his feet and pranced proudly back to the house. It might not have been the grandest house in the world, but by God, it was his territory, and he'd lay claim any way necessary.

Austin said, "In the glove box you will find a map." They drove along with the windows halfway down.

Emily was tired from staying up so late the night before. She was accustomed to staying up to all hours, but she was also accustomed to sleeping late. Emily unfolded the map and stared at the page. It was a hodgepodge of colors and lines, dots and names. It might as well have been hieroglyphics.

"I can't read a map," she said.

Austin was unsure if he heard her correctly. "Excuse me?"

"I can't read a map," Emily repeated.

Austin explained, "It's not a foreign language, it's a map. Everyone over the age of five has the ability to read a map. Now, what route do you wish to take through Texas?"

They were on the verge of their first real fight. Austin had little to no experience with the concept of a woman. He still believed arguments could be won, and right was right.

Emily turned her head and looked Austin in the face. "I told you I can't read a map, and I don't wanna learn."

Austin gripped the steering wheel with his black driving gloves. "We call it 'reading' a map, but it's not actually 'reading.' It's more like 'deciphering.'"

Emily suddenly hurled the map out the open window. Austin got a quick glance as the paper hit the face of the wind, and then he took a look in the rearview mirror to see the open map flying through interstate traffic, over a small white sports car and then under the wheels of a big truck.

They rode in silence. Austin was less angry than he was perplexed. Emily was less perplexed than she was tired. After a short while, she fell asleep, the wind from the half-open window swirling her light brown hair. Austin had never watched a beautiful woman sleep. He found himself looking at her freely, allowing himself to take in her knees, and then up to her thighs, at the very edge of the skirt. And her hands, small and thin, resting in her lap. Emily's face was smooth and tan, with just the tiniest of white hairs on her lip, something Austin had never imagined before. And her ears, hair tucked behind, decorated with little light-blue earrings.

It was an amazing thing. Austin struggled to keep his eyes on the road and his mind out of the gutter of lust. To be allowed to watch her sleep was more important than he had known, and then Emily began to snore lightly. It started as a peaceful breathing, in and out, a sign of deep rest, but it slowly built to something more. Emily reached full snore, loud like Curly on *The Three Stooges*, a sucking grunt, the inhale being the loudest, and then the exhale a flapping sound. It was hard for Austin to believe such a noise could come from this beautiful creature, but come it did, over and over, until he could stand it no more, and slammed on the brakes as part of an elaborate plan to avoid hitting a non-existent dog crossing the highway.

Emily awoke in a fright, her body whiplashed forward. Austin released the brakes and exclaimed, "That was close."

"What happened?" Emily asked. Her heart raced.

"We nearly hit a dog."

"Oh God, what kind of dog?" she asked.

Austin's plan lacked details. He said the first thing that came to his mind, "A basset hound, I think."

Emily looked back through the rearview mirror. "You hardly ever see basset hounds on the interstate."

"That's exactly what I was thinking," Austin replied. And then the blaring sound of a siren filled the air.

Austin looked in his rearview mirror. Beyond the cats he saw an Alabama highway patrol vehicle. The blue lights spun round and round on the top.

Austin stuck his tree-trunk arm out the window and waved the trooper around. "Certainly," he said, "he must be pursuing a fugitive up ahead." He squinted into the distance for any sign of a speeding car weaving in and out of traffic, but the trooper didn't go around, so Austin waved again.

"I think he wants you to pull over," Emily said.

"Surely not."

"I think so," she said.

Austin eased the car into the emergency lane and slowed to a stop. As Emily had suspected, the state trooper stopped behind them. They watched as the tall, crew-cut man walked from his vehicle, wearing black boots and sunglasses just like the movies. Austin felt the flutter of anxiety in his belly.

"May I see your license and registration, sir?"

Austin's license was in his wallet, and his wallet was in his back pants pocket. Without exiting the vehicle, removing his wallet would require great energy and mathematical precision.

"What's the problem, officer?"

"What's the problem? I'll tell you the problem. You nearly caused a pile-up on the interstate. That's the problem. You slammed on your brakes in heavy traffic."

Austin glanced at Emily. She came to his defense. "He was trying to keep from hitting a dog. We love animals. See?" she said, and pointed to the cats in the back window.

The officer looked inside the car. His trained

eye scanned for contraband and drug paraphernalia among the canned hams and other items in the backseat.

"I didn't see a dog, ma'am," the trooper said.

"Oh, yes," Emily shot back, "a basset hound. We barely missed it."

The trooper seemed to size up the situation. "Sir, I'll need you to step out of the vehicle and walk back with me to the patrol unit."

Austin opened the door and started the process. Cars whizzed by at what appeared to be incredible speeds. Finally Austin was out. He followed the trooper back to his car, removing his wallet and license on the way. The police officer sat in the driver's seat as Austin maneuvered into the passenger side, leaving the door ajar to accommodate his right leg.

The trooper looked at the license.

"Mr. McAdoo, you caused a dangerous situation. Your actions were reckless. I have no choice but to issue a citation."

Austin calmly countered, "I must tell you, if necessary, I shall contact the American Humane Society. I'm not so sure you wish to tangle with those people, if you know what I mean?"

The trooper once again seemed to take a moment to size up the situation. He slowly removed his sunglasses and looked Austin directly in the eyes. His face had become flushed and his nostrils dilated.

"Is that a threat?"

Austin swallowed. He looked at his car parked

ahead and saw Glenn watching his every move. That's when he heard a strange sound, almost like a tiny snort, a gurgling throatal sound. He turned to see the Alabama state trooper's eyes roll up into his head, and then his chin drop to his chest. There was quiet in the car.

Austin stared at the man for some time. He looked for any twitches of movement. Nothing. He bent down to look into the closed eyes. Nothing again.

"Hello," Austin whispered. No response.

"Hello," he said again. "Is this some type of trick?"

The police radio blared something about a broken-down motorist at mile marker 27.

Austin touched the trooper's leg with his index finger, pressing slightly, then harder, and still harder, to induce a reaction of some sort. The man was dead. There was no reaction, no breathing sounds, no twitches of movement. Nothing.

Finally, Austin McAdoo was left alone in a patrol car with a dead Alabama state trooper on the side of Interstate 20 outside of Tuscaloosa, Alabama. He pondered his options, and then panicked anyway. Austin got out of the car, closed the door gently, and hurried up to his little car as inconspicuously as possible.

Emily asked, "What happened?"

Austin took a long, deep breath, and said, "He just issued me a warning."

Emily smiled, "Well, that was nice of him."

Austin took another deep breath. "Yes, it was."

He started the car and merged into traffic. Approximately two miles down the road Austin remembered something horrible. His driver's license. It was in the police car, somewhere. It must have fallen out of the man's hand onto the floorboard. It must have dropped as the trooper lost consciousness and slipped into the abyss.

Austin's head spun. There could be an investigation. How would he explain his departure? Why hadn't he rendered assistance or used the police radio? But the man was dead, a victim of natural causes, God's will. Why wait around and risk being issued a reckless driving ticket, or cause delay to the journey, or get detained as a material witness, and wait for some idiot to finish the autopsy?

There was a road sign. "Highway 82 - Columbus." He took the exit.

Emily asked, "Do we need gas?"

"No," Austin said. "I just thought, if we are traveling the country, why not take the back highways? Interstates are the same wherever you go, but small highways criss-cross through small towns, farms. We should enjoy the flavor of America."

Emily smiled again. "That's a good idea."

The next sign said, "Columbus - 44 miles."

Austin felt sweat on his brow, and his horse-sized heart beat wildly within his chest. They should be discovering the dead man about now, he thought. Had the officer called in the license plate before they sat in the car together? And then Austin thought to himself, how strange it is that the man died when and where he died, but then again, with more than six billion people on the planet, and very few of us deciding when and where to die, perhaps it's more strange we don't see someone die around us each and every day.

"Look," Emily yelled, pointing to a sign up ahead.

The sign was white, with a huge rust-colored chicken painted in the middle. At the bottom it said, "SEE THE WORLD'S LARGEST CHICKEN— 2 MILES WEST OF REFORM, ALABAMA—YOU WON'T BELIEVE YOUR FREAKIN' EYES."

Both Emily Dooley and Austin McAdoo possessed vivid imaginations, although they were very different from each other. Both tried to envision the giant chicken. Emily imagined a docile Rhode Island Red the size of a Shetland pony sitting on a porch by a swing next to a sleeping bloodhound. Austin saw a Godzilla-sized man-killing chicken stomping on the roof of a barn and eating cows as if they were kernels of corn strewn in the yard, mooing and running from certain death.

"Do you think there's an admission price to view the chicken?" Austin asked.

"Who cares?" Emily answered. "I wanna see it."

Austin imagined the giant chicken swallowing Glenn whole and then dancing a little chicken-strut in celebration of the delicious snack. Austin turned off the road and followed the signs until they came upon a quaint farmhouse surrounded by lush pastures. He pulled into the gravel driveway and stopped. An old man came slowly around the back of the house. He wore overalls with no shirt underneath and a hat to block the sun from his eyes. His boots dragged over the ground.

"How do, folks?"

"We came to see the big chicken," Emily said excitedly.

"That'll be five dollars each." The old farmer spoke in a thick drawl.

Emily gave the man two five dollar bills, and they followed him to the backyard. The old farmer stopped in front of a big dusty patch of land between the house and the barn. There were twenty or thirty multicolored chickens leisurely pecking and walking around like chickens do. The farmer stood silent.

Austin and Emily looked across the yard, tilting and craning their necks in anticipation of the first glimpse of the huge bird, but the old man remained silent, hands in the pockets of his faded blue overalls.

"Where is it?" Austin finally asked.

The old man slowly removed his right hand from the deep pocket and pointed into the yard toward the twenty or thirty chickens in front of the barn.

Austin squinted. Emily tried to line up her sight with the pointed crooked finger like a gun barrel.

"There she is," the old farmer said, "the big red one."

In the yard of chickens, there was only one red, one slightly larger than the others. Austin squinted hard and shook his head from side to side. He was not a man to be duped.

Austin said, "We'll be taking our money back and going on our way, sir, and you'll be hearing from the Better Business Bureau within seventy-two hours."

The old man turned his head to look at Austin. His hand was still outstretched, pointing at his prized possession. "What's the problem?" he asked slowly.

Austin was ready. "The problem is, this is a scam. That chicken is not the world's largest chicken. It's not even close."

The old farmer asked, "Are you an expert on chickens?"

"No, sir, I am not, but I do not need formal poultry training to know that your chicken, the red chicken, certainly is not the world's largest chicken. I've seen bigger in the grocery store, frozen and ready for immediate consumption."

The old man lowered his hand and placed it back in the deep pocket. He looked out over his yard and then said, "I can't be held responsible for your imagination or your expectations. You probably pictured a chicken the size of Godzilla stompin' houses and eatin' folks. There ain't no chickens that big. There just ain't."

Emily looked at Austin. She flashed back to the image of the pony-sized chicken on the porch next to the dog, and she waited for Austin to say something.

"That's stupid," Austin said. "Everybody knows there are no chickens the size of Godzilla. We simply expected truth in advertising."

On the other side of the chicken yard, coming

around the side of the barn, something caught Austin's attention. He turned, and then Emily turned to see what he was staring at.

It was a chicken. A large, red chicken, about the size of a big beach ball. The animal had a strut like she owned the place, putting one steady foot out, touching the ground, pausing for a moment, and then shifting her weight forward to repeat the process. The farmer, Emily, and Austin watched the chicken strut to the other chickens and stand in the crowd. She stood tall, dwarfing the multicolored pitiful creatures around her.

The old man said, mostly to himself, "It's all about expectations, ain't it?"

Austin looked at the old farmer with his sunbaked skin and brown boots. He looked back at the chicken in the yard and wondered if it really might be the largest chicken in the entire world.

They drove the rest of the day on Highway 82 westbound through Mississippi and into Arkansas. They stopped for lunch, got gas, and even pulled over a few times to look at things or just stretch their legs.

Austin talked. "People act like they'd wish to live forever, but immortality is entirely overrated. The truth of the matter is this: if there was a recipe, an absolute, guaranteed recipe for immortality, people wouldn't follow it.

"For instance, let's say the scientific community

determined with certainty that a person could live indefinitely eating only onions and drinking only warm buffalo milk. How long do you think people would stick to it? How many would eat onions and drink warm buffalo milk every single day? Not many, I say.

"The longer a person lasted, the more they would realize a life without end is a life of onions and milk, endless. Even the strong would go for a piece of chocolate cake, or a glass of ice cold purple grape juice, or even a peanut.

"You see what I'm saying?"

Emily said, "I can't stop thinking about the big chicken."

Part Two

KENNETH MINT

"Life and love are life and love, a bunch of violets is a bunch of violets, and to drag the idea of a point is to ruin everything. Live and let live, love and let love, flower and fade, and follow the natural curve, which flows on pointless."

—*D.H. Lawrence*

CHAPTER 5

As night fell, it began to rain lightly. Ten miles outside of El Dorado, Arkansas, Austin pulled into a truck stop. He had high pressure in his bladder and a deep need to urinate as soon as possible. He parked the car at the gas pump and started inside. The rain fell a little harder.

The sign above read: Restrooms. The sign on the door read: Out of Order. There were four women in line for the ladies' room. The last one had a teardrop tattoo under her eye and a cigarette hanging from the edge of her lovely mouth.

Austin uttered, "This is ridiculous."

The man behind the counter said, "I just been pissin' around the side of the buildin'."

The word 'pissin' made Austin cringe. He said, "I imagine you have. It sounds like a delightful place to piss." And he cringed again at the word.

Emily entered and took her place in line. Austin chose not to explain in detail.

"I will wait for you outside."

Emily smiled. The cold rain stung Austin's back and shoulders. He hugged the side of the building and turned the corner from fluorescent brightness to back-alley dark. With his right hand he reached out to touch the brick wall and kept his finger on the wall as he walked further down the side of the building, careful not to go too fast. Finally, he reached the end and found a spot in the darkness he felt was safely hidden from any passersby.

Austin unzipped and began to urinate. He squinted but was unable to see that he was standing on the edge of a hill, his feet positioned perfectly at the precipice, a muddy slope only inches from the tips of his toes. The rain fell. In the darkness, his eyes adjusting poorly and the sound of the rain in the trees, Austin lost perspective and leaned a bit forward. With penis in hand, he stepped out to brace himself and found no earth below his foot where he expected earth to be.

The enormous man lost his balance, threw his hands up to catch himself, landed with a thump, and proceeded to roll down the muddy hill, penis flying free, rolling and rolling over and over again, until he finally came to rest with a thud against the wheel of a single-wide trailer owned by Gladys Welch and her common-law husband, Parnell. Both heard the sound and felt the trailer shake, but neither reacted to the distraction as they made good love on the floor in front of the flickering TV.

Austin raised his head to look up the hill at the faint fluorescent light above. There was dirt in every orifice and all exposed skin was scratched and scraped. He lay still for minutes listening to the gentle moans of Gladys and Parnell and the rhythm of the squeaky trailer floor. He was unfamiliar with the sounds of lovemaking.

"Perhaps," he thought, "this is much like hell," and then felt a sharp pain from his private area.

If not for the thought of Emily and her fear at not finding him, Austin may have simply remained against the wheel of the trailer and waited to die. Instead, he gathered his strength and stood like Bigfoot in the woods. Every bone hurt.

Curiosity got the best of him, and he peeked in the trailer window to see Parnell's naked ass rise and fall like the Roman Empire.

"God help me," Austin whispered.

Austin zipped his pants and headed up the hill in the rain, step by excruciating step, grasping bushes, low tree limbs, and anything else along the way. Slipping, sliding,
falling, and losing a shoe at one point, only later to discover the shoe stuck inside his pants leg.

Emily finally got to use the bathroom. She bought two Ding-Dongs and a quart of buttermilk and stepped out into the rain. Austin was nowhere to be seen, and she stood in the doorway wondering where he may have gone.

Kenneth Mint was pretending to be interested in the confederate flag cigarette lighters in the display case as he watched Emily. He'd been in the truck stop seventeen straight hours since his car died on the highway and he walked the half-mile to his current location. He had no money, no one to come get him, and very little hope of securing transportation without trickery or deceit. He was a thirty-year-old white disgruntled traveling semi-preacher who doubted the existence of everything, including himself, but felt strongly anyway about certain things. He'd watched with interest Austin McAdoo enter and leave.

Austin emerged from around the side of the building. Emily recognized the form. Two men were exiting their brown pickup truck between Emily and Austin. One of them, the one with the dirty green shirt, said to Austin, "Damn, boy, you outta stay out of the pig trough."

When Emily turned and walked to her right, Kenneth Mint seized the opportunity, grabbed his small suitcase, and walked briskly out the door to the red car parked at the pump. He climbed in the backseat and covered himself with anything available. Desperation is the mother.

Emily heard the men laugh. The switch clicked in her brain. The carton of buttermilk exploded against the man's head. Emily's fingernails dug into the skin of his cheek. The man let out a howl, and Austin stood in amazement. Kenneth Mint heard the scream and raised his eyes above the passenger headrest to see beautiful Emily Dooley running across the parking lot, hand in hand with a gigantic mud-man.

It was too late to get out of the car. For better or worse, he had made his decision, and anything was better than one more minute in the truck stop smelling chili he couldn't eat.

The man with the dirty green shirt cussed. "Crazy bitch." He chased Austin and Emily a few steps and then turned around to get a shotgun out from behind the seat of the pickup. His borderline retarded friend said, "What you doing?"

"I'm gonna shoot somebody," he yelled.

Austin hit the gas, and the little red car spun in a circle and out to the highway. Emily's rage had settled, and they were both out of breath. Austin raced down the road toward El Dorado. Kenneth Mint smelled something rancid in his hiding place only a few inches from his nose. Glenn's ass happened to be nearby. Kenneth rose up suddenly. Emily turned and screamed. Austin looked in the rearview mirror and screamed himself. Kenneth sat perfectly still and said calmly, "What are you two doing in my new car?"

Emily screamed again. The cats were frantic, darting this way and that. Austin began to pull the car to the side of the road.

Kenneth said, "Don't pull over. The man in the pickup truck is chasing you."

Austin looked past the stranger's head in the mirror and saw headlights in the distance. It looked like a truck. He imagined the driver, buttermilk dripping in lines down his face, shotgun in his lap, seeking revenge.

Austin veered back on the highway and pressed the accelerator.

"Sir," Austin said sternly, "carjacking is a serious crime."

The mud on Austin's face was hardening into a shell. Emily kept her eyes on the man in the backseat.

"I'm not a carjacker. In fact, it's very much the other way around."

Emily said, "You're not right. This is our car. We're on a trip, and as soon as we get to the next town we're going straight to the police station."

"I wouldn't do that if I was you," Kenneth said. He smiled at Austin like he knew something, and Austin wondered how the strange man in the backseat of the car could possibly know about the dead state trooper.

The truck didn't seem to be gaining on them. Austin couldn't even be sure it was the buttermilk man, but now he had to find a way not to involve the police.

"Are you armed?" Austin asked hesitantly.

"Of course not, although I believe in the Biblical right to bear arms."

"Why are you in our car?" Austin asked.

"I need a ride to Los Angeles. The world is coming to a natural and sinful conclusion, and Los Angeles is the place I'm supposed to be when it takes place. I don't know where you're supposed to be."

Emily interrupted, "Stop talking to him," she said to Austin, "I want him out."

She watched as Glenn slowly and unexpectedly climbed down from his perch in the back window and into the lap of Kenneth Mint. Emily could hear the cat purring. Glenn never took to strangers in such a way.

She said in a low voice, almost to herself, "He likes you."

"Yes," Kenneth said, "animals have a strong sense of goodness. I am a man of the Lord, a traveling preacher, and I'm over ninety-five percent goodness. The other five percent consists of bad cholesterol and a pornography temptation, but both are in check. I don't eat red meat."

Emily and Austin looked at each other.

Kenneth said, "Can you think of anything scarier than a monkey with a switchblade? Think about it. It's scary enough when a regular person has a switchblade, but a monkey doesn't even know the difference between right and wrong. He doesn't know the law."

Emily said, "You're a weird man. Monkeys don't have switchblades. They don't have any money to buy anything."

"This is true. Are you two married?"

"No," Austin answered.

"Not yet," Emily said, and then smiled for the first time since the strange man appeared in the backseat of the car. She caught herself and frowned immediately.

"Well, I'm licensed in the great state of California to perform marriages. Maybe a little ceremony on

Hollywood Boulevard. What do you say, mud-man?"

In all the excitement, Austin had forgotten his shell of mud. He stretched his face and felt the cracks form in the coating.

Emily said, "We need to find a motel and clean you up."

Kenneth replied, "Thanks, but I prefer to sleep in the car."

Emily didn't know what to say. She was unsure why Austin wasn't demanding that the strange man go away, but she sure liked the idea of a wedding on Hollywood Boulevard. Emily could imagine standing on the sidewalk star of Julia Roberts, her favorite movie star, in a beautiful white wedding dress next to Austin McAdoo in his black tuxedo. She said the name to herself, Emily Marie McAdoo, and then looked down at Glenn, his chin pointed upward in delight, as the man stroked the cat's throat.

"There's a motel," Emily pointed.

Austin saw no headlights in the rearview mirror. He turned the car swiftly, without a blinker, in case the green-shirted man was still somewhere behind.

After checking into the motel and parking the car in front of room 11, Kenneth offered, "You can leave the cats out here. I'll take care of 'em."

Emily said, "No."

Austin liked the idea, especially after the last motel-cat experience concluded with mace. "Well, perhaps that's not such a bad idea. The lady said, 'No pets,' and Glenn seems uncomfortable inside."

Austin glanced at Kenneth in time to see Kenneth wink at him like they were together, partners in conspiracy, and in the bright light from the motel, Austin thought he recognized the odd man. Kenneth Mint was tall and lean with wavy short red hair, a bird-like face, and hairless arms. He was not tired in the slightest, having slept in the truck stop lounge for twelve of the seventeen hours of captivity, stretched out with his hands neatly folded across his chest like a corpse.

"O.K.," Emily finally agreed and then gritted her teeth and said, "but I'll be out to check on the boys every few hours."

Kenneth watched the huge mud-covered man and the volatile little woman amble up to the motel room door, suitcases in hand, and then disappear inside. Glenn sniffed Kenneth's only suitcase, a small brown jobby with a broken handle.

"I know what you're sniffin'."

Kenneth opened the suitcase and pulled out a hideous coat made of woven human hair. It was the only thing Kenneth had gotten from his grandmother after she died. He remembered her long flowing gray hair as he held the coat in his hands and made a pillow to lean his head. He found comfort in her memory.

The next morning, Austin looked down at the muddy bathtub and felt no remorse for the mess. His pores were open and free, and the memory of the sight of Parnell Welch's naked body seemed distant and unreal.

Kenneth did his washing-up early at the hose by the green pool and used the lobby bathroom. He wasn't about to abandon the car while Austin and Emily were around and provide the opportunity to be left behind.

Somehow, Austin had been successful the night before persuading Emily to allow the strange man to ride along for awhile. Each had their own reasons, reasons purposefully planted by Kenneth Mint himself in his subtle manipulation with Glenn, the marriage scenario, and the threat of contacting the police. "Desperation may be the mother," Kenneth thought, "but manipulation is the provider."

He stuck his hand out the door toward Austin with an invitation to shake.

"I apologize for the lack of a proper introduction. My name is Kenneth."

Austin introduced himself and Emily. They all prepared for the next leg of the journey.

"What kind of coat is that?" Emily asked, her face squinted.

"It's a coat of human hair, my grandmother's hair, and it's warmer than any coat in the world. Warmer than beaver."

Austin kept glaring in the rearview mirror, trying to size-up in the daylight the odd fellow. He knew he recognized him from somewhere, but he couldn't place the long bird-face.

After a few minutes of silence, Kenneth said, "I just want to spend one minute on the sun. That's all I ask. One minute."

Austin waited a moment after Emily glanced at him, and slowly explained, as if to a child, "Well, that's not possible. Millions of miles before reaching the sun you'd explode into flames. You can't go there. Not even for a minute."

"I'm aware. I'm speaking metaphorically. Of course I'd explode into flames in reality. But this isn't reality, is it? So I can go there for a minute if I can only find transportation. Will you take me in this little red rocket ship?"

Austin glanced in the mirror again. He finally said, "Kenneth, I believe you suffer from a mental illness of some sort. It may be very treatable."

Kenneth Mint laughed. "Ahh, I thought you might say that. You're a man who lives in a box of your own making. You're unable to see beyond ham, and cats, and your next buffet."

Austin was offended by the 'buffet' comment, but tried to hide his brief anger.

Kenneth continued, "Imagine for a moment you are a green pea. One small green pea in a can on a shelf in one supermarket in one American town. Say, Corkdale, Missouri, for instance."

Emily's eyes were pointed forward. They widened, and she shook her head slightly from side to side, sending a message to Austin.

"Now, you're crammed inside this can, drowning

in your own juices, listening to all the other peas talk about religion and philosophy, patriotism and politics. The peas are saying this and that, and the drone of their voices puts you in a trance. A thinking trance. And you come up with this brilliant idea to escape from the can, steal a tiny car, and drive to St. Louis, but none of the other peas will listen to what you have to say. You can't execute the complicated plan alone, so what do you do? You give up. That's what you do. You give up and go back to listening to all the crap the other peas have to say."

Emily turned to face the man in the backseat. "That's so stupid. There aren't any little cars like that at the supermarket."

Kenneth smiled. "You got it. You understand. Now, I must urinate. It is a fundamental requirement of being alive. Please don't watch. I shall shake it only three times at the conclusion without concern for you or your ethnic background. Pull over here, please."

The car came to a stop.

"Don't be alarmed. I'll take Glenn with me. It's the only way I can be sure you won't leave and steal my grandmother's coat."

Emily blurted out, "We don't want your grand-mother's coat."

When Kenneth was behind the tree thirty yards away, Emily whispered, "He's very weird, but I can't believe how much Glenn likes him. Animals have a sense for people. Maybe he's like a prophet or something?"

Austin considered arguing in favor of driving away and leaving Glenn and Kenneth behind, but decided not to bring it up. He imagined Kenneth sitting in a police station with the cat in his lap, selecting Austin's picture from a photographic lineup of murderers and pedophiles.

Back in the car, they rode in silence for fifteen minutes down Highway 82 into Texas. Kenneth said, "You like pilgrims, Austin?"

He said it like it didn't mean a thing. Austin continued to study the man in the mirror.

Emily answered, "I like pilgrims. I don't like their clothes, but I like the pilgrims themselves."

Kenneth asked again, "What about you, Austin?"

The face, the wavy red hair, the eyes, he looked familiar but Austin still couldn't place him.

Kenneth said, "When I was in the third grade, Miss Perkins, the teacher, decided to have a special day we would all dress like pilgrims.

"One little boy's mother dressed him to the hilt. Black pilgrim shoes, the hat, the vest, right down to the big pilgrim belt. She drove him to school in the family car and dropped him off in front."

Austin and Kenneth's eyes were locked in the mirror.

"Unfortunately, for the kid, it was the wrong day. His mother was a week early, and she drove off just about the time the kid walked behind the building to the playground and saw every finger point at him. Heard every kid laugh at the stupid pilgrim shoes and the ridiculous pilgrim belt."

It all came back to Austin like an avalanche. He saw himself, the fattest little pilgrim, all alone, ground zero of ridicule, and he could still see the back of his mother's family car driving away down the street.

Austin said, "You're Kenneth Mint. Little Kenny Mint."

"And you're Austin McAdoo, the pilgrim."

Emily turned and inserted the top half of her body into the backseat until her nose touched Kenneth's nose. Her eyes shot fire as her index finger touched the skin of the man's cheek.

She growled, "Did you laugh at him?"

Kenneth sat still.

"Answer the question," Emily yelled.

Kenneth said, "A little bit," and then pointed out the window at a sign. He read out loud, "WORLD'S LARGEST CHICKEN—TURN LEFT NOW—GO 1 MILE."

"Where?" Emily spun her head around. "Where?"

The sign showed another big red chicken, much like the one they'd seen before.

"Turn," she yelled.

Austin was thankful to think of something besides the terrible pilgrim episode. He'd been haunted by it for years, but the memory had slowly faded. Now, on the journey of his lifetime, a strange man invades the backseat of the car at a truck stop in Arkansas in the rain and it turns out to be little Kenny Mint, the crazy kid who twisted the legs off of dragonflies so they couldn't land.

Austin pulled the car into a trailer park. A Mexican kid, maybe six years old, sat in a folding chair by the front door of a dilapidated white trailer. Above the kid was a hand-painted sign: SEE BIG CHICKEN—$5.

Austin, Emily, and Kenneth stood in the hot Texas sun. Emily gave the kid fifteen dollars. The kid led the way down a dusty path to a clearing. Kenneth still held the cat in his arms. In the center of the clearing stood a wooden shack. The boy led the group to the door of the shack. He turned around and said, in broken English, "Da beeg cheeken is meen. Look quick."

The boy swung open the door to reveal a red chicken, approximately the size of a full-grown pig, sitting alone on the dirt floor, perfectly still. The sunlight shone through a hole in the roof like a spotlight.

The boy swung the door back and slammed it closed.

Kenneth said, "That wasn't real."

"What?" Emily asked.

"It wasn't real. It was a big fake stuffed chicken. A piñata."

Kenneth reached to open the door, and the boy struggled to stop him.

"No, señor, no. Da cheeken is very meen."

Kenneth managed to grab the doorknob with his free hand and opened the door wide. There was a split-second when Austin and Emily thought Kenneth was right. It was a big fake stuffed chicken. A piñata maybe filled with candy treats. But then the animal stood, wide and solid on its two thin legs, and turned to face the open door. The chicken charged, like a beast from the flames of Hell, all red eyes and beak, flying feathers and chicken feet slapping dust.

The boy was the first to run, then Kenneth and Emily, with Austin McAdoo last, lumbering through the clearing down the dirt path. He could feel the giant bird's beak pecking the backs of his legs, the white skin turning red, a bad day to wear shorts.

The bird was relentless. Austin knew if he fell to the ground he would face certain death, or at least blindness, or the loss of an ear.

Up ahead Austin could see Kenneth and then Emily dive in the car. Emily reached across and opened the driver's door. There would be no time for the usual car-entry ritual. There would be no time for the squat, the clockwise turn, the push back into position.

Austin seized the door handle, dove headlong inside across the console, still feeling the pecking pain on his bare ankles above his socks. Austin squeezed back, rolled slightly, reached his left hand to the inside door handle, and pulled the car door shut with all his power. The giant chicken's head was crushed like a walnut. His body folded to the ground and lay lifeless.

Austin slammed the door, fumbled for the keys, finally started the car, and spun his tires in the gravel of the trailer park driveway. The Mexican boy and two men, one with a blue bandana, ran from the trailer toward Austin's car. The one with the bandana picked up a rock and threw it at the car and struck the back window, the glass cracking like a spiderweb but remaining intact.

"Oh my God. Oh my God," Emily repeated. "Oh my God. We killed the chicken. We killed the chicken."

"That was no chicken," Kenneth said. "That was Satan himself in the form of a chicken."

Austin screamed, "You're the same person who said it was a piñata. You let it out. It wanted to kill us."

He wheeled the car around a corner, back on Highway 82 westbound, ten miles outside of Detroit, Texas. Emily started to cry softly. Blood oozed from the sore spots on the backs of Austin's creamy legs. A single rust-colored chicken feather came loose from the door jamb, swept up on a gust of wind from the open window, and landed gently on the dashboard, swirling gracefully in circles.

"Sorry," Kenneth said.

CHAPTER 6

Austin finally found a pay telephone at a gas station outside of St. Jo, Texas. He called his mother collect, something he'd done many times in his life.

"Austin, what the hell have you done?"

"What do you mean?"

"The police were here yesterday. Scared the bajesus out of Lafitte."

Austin felt a weakness in his legs. For his entire life, Austin McAdoo held a gothic fear of law enforcement authorities. His psychiatrist attributed this unfounded fear to a toxic combination of childhood instability, watching too much television, and a mistrust of a male neighbor named Perry.

"What did they want?"

Lila McAdoo took another drag from her cigarette and said, "Hell, I couldn't tell. They never would come out and say. Something to do with your driver's license. What in God's name did you do?"

Austin looked over at his car by the gas pump thirty yards away. He could see Emily saying something to Kenneth Mint in the backseat, but Austin couldn't hear Kenneth answer, "No, ma'am. I'm a member of the congregation of the Holy Church of Divine Deprivation. We don't have an actual physical location, but we share the unwavering belief that deprivation is the key to salvation. I sleep only in uncomfortable locations. I remain celibate, own less than five worldly possessions at any given moment, and eat as little as possible, and when I do eat, it's something of poor nutritional value."

Emily perked up. "I once went two days without a single bite of food." She repeated, "Two days."

Austin asked his mother, "Did they search the house?"

She answered, "No, why? Did you put something nasty under your bed again?"

"Mother, this is serious. How did you get them to leave?"

"Well, I told the cute one I had a stolen gun in my panties, and he had a duty to collect the evidence."

"Jesus Christ, Mother."

"Oh, yeah," she said, "I also told them you were dead."

"Dead?"

Lila said, "Speaking of dead, you know what you should do on your big trip? You should stop by and see your father in Las Vegas."

Austin was confused. "You told me my father passed away."

"He did, you idiot. You should go by and see his grave. It would be a cathartic experience, cleanse your conscience. Hell, who knows, it might free you from all your crazy-ass fears."

In the car, Kenneth said to Emily, "I see the way you look at Austin. Have you figured out why you feel the way you feel?"

Emily turned her head to look at Austin McAdoo outside on the pay phone. She smiled at him.

"There's nothing to figure out," Emily said.

Kenneth continued, "You know, for lots of people, there's this one person in their life who does it for them. Most of the time, it's that one person who comes along at exactly the right time in your life, and then disappears before you can get to know them long enough for the shine to fade. They exist in your mind with a haze."

Emily continued to look at Austin as she listened to the man in the backseat. There was a moment of silence as she thought about what he said.

Finally, Emily said, "I feel sorry for those people."

Austin wondered why she continued to stare at him.

His mother said on the other end of the phone, "Somebody named Cremora called. She said she was trying to get in touch with Emily. I told her where you were. She sounded like a lesbian. How is she involved in your new life as a fugitive?"

"I'm not a fugitive, Mother. It's just a misunder-standing."

Lila said, "Like the misunderstanding with Mr. Triola when you ran over the hedges."

"Yes," Austin exclaimed. "Much the same. And for once, maybe you could support my position."

Lila McAdoo purposefully dropped a piece of crust from her burnt toast to the kitchen floor next to the poodle. Lafitte turned and walked away in disgust.

"Austin, have you figured out yet why that beautiful girl ran off with you?"

He looked back at the car and Emily was still watching him. She had a sad look on her face, and Austin hoped crazy Kenneth Mint wasn't poisoning the miracle.

"I've gotta go, Mother. I'll call you from Las Vegas." He hung up.

A few minutes later, Austin and Kenneth ended up in the gas station bathroom together. They stood next to each other at the urinals, separated by nothing. Both men looked dead ahead at the gray wall in front.

The silence was interrupted by a shrill whistling sound.

Austin glanced just slightly to his right and then straightened his gaze.

"What was that?" he asked.

"What was what?" Kenneth said.

And then the sound came again. A shrill, quick

whistling sound, cut off in mere seconds, with no lingering after-sound.

"That noise. What is that noise?"

Kenneth answered, "Oh, that noise. It's a butt whistle. My heart medication causes gas buildup. I had a butt whistle surgically implanted. It helps me know I'm alive."

Austin contemplated the idea. There was a great deal of information in only a few sentences. It didn't seem physically possible, and then he heard the sound for the third time.

Kenneth said, "That girl, Emily, she's really got it bad for you. What did you do?"

Austin had never really had man-to-man talks in his life. There was no father, or older brother, or drinking buddy. Austin was leery of sharing his bewilderment.

"I don't understand your question," he said.

"Sure you do. Guys like you and me, we're lucky if a good-looking woman talks to us at all. We dream about 'em, think about 'em, hoist 'em up on impossible pedestals, but it's not often one of them falls head-over-heels for a guy like you and me. What did you do? Hypnotize her? Is she hypnotized?"

"No."

Austin walked to the sink to wash his hands. He noticed Kenneth standing at the door ready to leave.

"Aren't you going to wash your hands?" Austin asked.

"You must be kidding. Do you read the newspaper? Haven't you seen the germ research on public bathrooms? There's more germs in the water from that public sink than in your own urine. You might as well wash your hands in the toilet. And the paper towels, the brown towels, there's more bacteria per square inch than on your penis. The most sanitary thing you can do in a place like this is shove your hands in your pockets and leave."

Austin looked closely at the rusted silver faucet and imagined the pipes beneath filled with hair and drowned roaches. He reached up for a paper towel and caught himself. On the edge of the towel, almost too small to detect, Austin saw a tiny stain. Kenneth noticed Austin's hesitation and was pleased.

Kenneth asked, "What time is it?"

Austin shook his hands to dry. "I have no idea."

"You're wearing a watch."

"So what. Time is relative, not stagnant like a puddle of water. And by the way, I don't believe your story of a surgically implanted butt whistle."

Kenneth Mint shrugged his shoulders, turned around, and the shrill sound came again from his pants. Kenneth waited by the door for Austin to walk past him. He said, "I hope you don't have any ideas about leaving me. I'd hate for Emily to find out about you know what."

Austin remembered little Kenny Mint from homeroom. He was the kid who terrorized the class, always carrying rodents in his pockets, or lighting things on fire. Surely someone had to know he would grow up to plague society. Surely the warning signs were apparent, Austin thought. What did Kenneth Mint know? Was it a bluff?

In the car, heading west, on a particularly boring stretch of Texas countryside, Austin McAdoo felt Emily Dooley's hand slide gently into his. It didn't just sit there. She squeezed, and held just enough pressure for their skin to touch comfortably. Austin swallowed and gripped the steering wheel tightly with his left hand. He squeezed back. Not too much, but just enough.

From the backseat there was the sound of pills shaken in a pill bottle. Kenneth said, "Tomorrow's the Fourth of July. We've got to stop and get some fireworks."

Emily bounced up and down in her seat like a schoolgirl.

"Can we? Can we? I've never shot fireworks before."

"I thought everybody shot fireworks," Kenneth said.

"I haven't," Austin admitted, and he looked at Emily, both of them happy to accidentally stumble across another thing they had in common.

Emily looked in the backseat to see Kenneth pop a yellow pill into his dry mouth.

"Hey, what was that?" she asked.

"Heart medication." He held up the prescription bottle for her to see.

"What's the matter with you?" she asked.

"I've got a bad ticker. Born with it. Crazy. A guy like Austin there, probably three hundred and fifty pounds, out of shape, probably got a perfect heart. Me, thin, don't eat red meat, a believer in God, and I never know whether the damn thing might just stop in the middle of a tick. Just give up. It's hard to plan for an uncertain future, so I never do."

The butt whistle went off, and Austin realized he heard it a few minutes earlier, but with the wind from an open window, and the sound of the engine, he hadn't paid much attention to the noise.

"What was that sound?" Emily asked.

"I didn't hear anything," Kenneth said. "How much you weigh, Austin?"

Austin squeezed up his face in dissatisfaction. "I don't see how that's relevant."

Kenneth said, "If you weigh three hundred and fifty pounds or more you can qualify for government obesity assistance. You can sit back on your couch, eat Oreos all day, watch Oprah, and wait for the mailman to bring your check to pay for more Oreos, a bigger couch, and a fancy new TV."

"I don't weigh three hundred and fifty pounds," Austin said.

"Well, you're close," Kenneth continued. "It would be worth it to pack on five or ten extra pounds for the check. How much you weigh, Emily?"

"I'm not tellin'."

Kenneth said, "I'm guessin' one hundred and ten.

Austin, I'm guessin' three hundred and forty-seven pounds, easy."

Austin was flabbergasted. He weighed exactly three hundred and forty-seven pounds. For a moment, more like a full minute, Austin considered the possibility of adding three extra pounds to his frame to qualify for the government obesity assistance.

Emily said, "Look! There's a fireworks stand."

Garrett and Katrina Boyle sat behind the counter. A box fan, secured in the window of the trailer with duct tape, blew a hot Texas breeze over the fireworks display. Emily, Austin, and Kenneth stood in front of the colorful table of cherry bombs, black cats, and crimson bottle rockets. As a child Emily never stepped foot in a fireworks stand, much less lit a fuse. Garrett Boyle had great difficulty removing his eyes from Emily's candy apple miniskirt. His wife noticed and laid a backhand hard against Garrett's big forehead, knocking his baseball cap to the floor.

"Shit, Katrina, what you do that for?" But he knew what it was for, and didn't care anyhow, and leaned down to pick up the baseball cap, already planning to sneak another peek in the wide open daylight. It was worth it.

"These are good," Kenneth said. "These are real good. They spin around in circles on the sidewalk and then take off like flying saucers, all gold sparks and stuff."

He showed a pack to Emily.

"Do you have any money?" Austin asked with a

purposeful pointed tone.

Before Kenneth could answer, two county sheriff's deputies stepped up into the trailer. Austin and Kenneth turned to see them at the same time, and then Kenneth said, still holding the pack of flying saucers in his hand, "What did you say?"

Austin felt the breath catch in his lungs. His meaty knees locked, and Austin felt a wave of lightness. He teetered slightly, blinked his eyes twice, and then fell headlong across the fireworks table, snapping the spindly wooden table legs beneath, crashing to the floor like a sack of sand dropped from a high roof.

"Holy crap," Garrett Boyle yelled.

Katrina fell over backwards in her chair. Kenneth let out an involuntary short burst of laughter and then stopped himself. Only Emily sprung to Austin's aid. She crawled across his massive back to the head area.

"Honey, honey," Emily first said, and then she wheeled around to the deputies and yelled with great force, "Do something."

The deputies, trained at the police academy to respond to orders, responded as ordered. One called an ambulance on his shoulder radio and the other prepared himself mentally for the possibility of giving the large victim mouth-to-mouth resuscitation. Before any such resuscitation efforts could commence, Austin awoke.

It wasn't the first time he'd fainted.

Austin said in a woozy voice, "It's the heat… need air…need clean air."

Garrett Boyle hadn't failed to seize the opportunity to look up Emily's skirt as she squatted over the semi-conscious giant. His wife picked herself up off the floor and again belted her husband, this time in the belly, causing Garrett to bend over at the waist. In the commotion, Kenneth stuck a package of bottle rockets under his shirt along with two other choice packages of unique explosives. He backpedaled out the door to the car where he hid his stash under the coat of hair.

The deputies lifted Austin to his unsteady feet. Emily held him like a child wrapping her arms around the trunk of a tree. They helped Austin walk outside where it was equally hot but less stuffy.

Austin McAdoo insisted he was all right and pleaded to be led to the vehicle. After he was assisted into a seated position on the passenger side, Emily, who'd failed her driving test twice, took the driver's position.

Emily said, "Thank you, officers. I'll take care of him. We'll open the windows and get some air on him. You'll be O.K., Austin."

Kenneth just gave a smile and a wave, pulling Glenn into position on top of the hair coat.

Garrett Boyle, after he recovered from the belly blow, said, "Hey, what about my table?" but it was too late. The red car was already on the road.

Emily hunched against the leather steering wheel and concentrated. Austin took three long, deep breaths in a row, regaining his faculties.

Kenneth said, "Wow, that was a close one."

Emily didn't hear what he said, and Austin ignored it.

"I got us some pretty good fireworks for tonight. We'll have our own little Fourth of July show," Kenneth said, and then Austin heard the whistling sound again. The thought made him nauseous and brought a sour taste into the back of his mouth.

Emily kept the speedometer on forty-five as cars flew around her as if she were sitting still. They drove to Lubbock on Highway 82 and switched to Highway 84, driving through the afternoon to a motel outside of Littlefield, Texas near the New Mexico border. Emily put a cool rag on Austin's forehead, and he took a two-hour nap in the air-conditioned room. At nightfall, the three sat out by the small pool and ate canned ham. They drank cold Cokes, and the cats laid around licking themselves like cats do. Austin bought a new map and studied the route.

He said, "Did you know there's a Las Vegas in New Mexico?"

Emily asked, "Is New Mexico part of the United States?"

"Yes," Austin answered quickly, not looking up from the map.

"What's new about it?" Emily innocently asked, chewing a nice bite of ham.

Austin wasn't sure how to answer. Instead, he said, "My father is buried in Las Vegas, but I'm not sure if it's Las Vegas, Nevada, or Las Vegas, New Mexico. I'll have to call my mother in the morning. I'd like to stop by and see his grave. I've never seen it."

"That's sweet," Emily said, and she looked at Austin with special eyes.

Kenneth turned off all the lights around the pool. In the darkness, he set up at the far end of the pool for his fireworks display. He decided to use the empty Coke bottle as a launcher for the rockets. Emily couldn't wait to begin.

"Can I light the first one? Can I light it?" she begged.

Kenneth placed the red-sticked rocket in the bottle and pulled the fuse outward for easy access. He handed the green cigarette lighter to Emily. She knelt down carefully, glanced back at Austin sitting at the table, and flicked the lighter. In the glow, Emily leaned over to touch the flame to the fuse. The fuse ignited and Emily backed away, wide-eyed, like a child.

The flame shot from the end of the rocket, rose slightly, and then flew into the starry Texas sky with a screech, exploding high above.

Emily squealed, and Austin couldn't help but smile at her excitement.

"Come on, Austin, you do the next one," she said.

Normally, Austin McAdoo would have said, "No." He would have said it quickly and refused to consider changing his mind. But now, on the Fourth of July, outside of Littlefield, Texas, next to a motel pool, he got up from the white metal chair and went to light his first bottle rocket.

Austin got down on one knee next to Emily.

Kenneth inserted the rocket in the launcher. Austin held the lighter near the fuse. He could feel his hand shake, and the others could see it in the glow of the green lighter.

Like the one before, the fuse ignited, the rocket spiraled into the sky, and the explosion drifted away.

Later, with Kenneth orchestrating the pyrotechnic display, Austin and Emily sat at the table side by side. They watched the spinning golden flying saucers and bottle rockets sent upward two at a time. They followed the small flames from the poolside into the air and waited for the pop at the end.

Emily leaned her head on Austin's shoulder. She lifted her face up to his, stretched, and touched her warm, soft lips to his cheek. Austin's heart rushed with the touch, and he became conscious of the dryness in his mouth. Emily felt flush with a warmth like her entire body was submerged in a bath. And then they kissed, a brush of her lips on his, and then a full kiss, gentle and remarkable. Much better than even their hopes or imaginations. Their lips parted, and both of them were left with the wonderful knowledge they would be allowed to do it again soon, and then again.

"Happy Fourth of July," Austin said.

"Happy Fourth of July," she answered.

They sat around the pool until deep into the night. Austin was tired, but he was anxious at the prospect of going back to the motel room and being alone with

Emily. Both were virgins, for very different reasons, and yet both assumed, also for very different reasons, the other to be more experienced in the ways of sex.

Kenneth told a story. "Do you remember, in Miss Perkins' class, the first day of school, do you remember what she did?"

"No," Austin answered.

"She leaned down and whispered in the ear of the first kid on the first row. She told him a secret, and then she told him to turn around and whisper the secret in the ear of the kid behind him, and so on and so on. The secret traveled up the row, and then down the next, from one kid's mouth to the next kid's ear.

"And you know what? When it got to the last girl, a girl named Lois, Miss Perkins asked her to stand up and tell the secret. And then the first kid who heard the secret was asked to stand up and tell us what he was told by the teacher at the beginning.

"It was completely different. The secret was a completely different secret. It made me wonder where it had all gone wrong. Did one stupid kid mess up the whole thing? Or did the words and the message slowly deteriorate along the way and slowly become something altogether different?

"I think that's what happened with the Bible. So many millions upon millions of people, telling and retelling the same stories, tweaking the messages with their own personal tweaks, until it's impossible to ever know what the original authors meant, or expected, without going back to the original authors themselves.

But we can't, they're all dead, so I guess we're stuck with the secret of Lois.

"I remember she was embarrassed for some reason. She was embarrassed because the kids laughed at her, but in the end, nobody could figure out who was to blame."

Austin and Emily listened to the whole story. Austin remembered Lois. She lived down the block from him, and everybody said she didn't wear underwear.

"Have you always been like this?" Emily asked Kenneth.

"What do you mean?"

"Have you always ridden around in people's backseats and told stories and slept in cars with hair coats, like now? I'm not trying to be mean. I was just wonderin'."

It was quiet outside. July fourth had become July fifth. The blanket of stars stretched from one horizon to the next. Kenneth dissected the question.

"No. I was married. Had a house. Twenty-seven hundred square feet. And a job at Blackwell Computer. I kept my clothes in drawers and wore uncomfortable shoes like everybody else."

"What happened?" Emily asked. "Did you have a nervous breakdown?"

Kenneth's hands fidgeted on the white tabletop. He told the usual semi-lie. "I guess you can call it whatever you want. Basically, I got tired of a lot of different things at the same time, instead of spread out over years.

"Like some people, I worked real hard to establish a daily, weekly, routine. And then I woke up one day in the middle of the routine, and I couldn't figure out anything. I couldn't figure out my wife, or my job, or the mortgage payment, or the phone bill, or why my insurance kept going up, or why I had to see the dentist every six months for the rest of my life when nothing was wrong with my teeth, or why the dog looked at me like he did. And even worse than not being able to figure out all those things, I really didn't give a shit anymore. It reached a certain point, I can't tell you exactly when, but after that point it was just too late.

"So they told me I was crazy, and I'd always been crazy, and I just needed a little medicine to balance everything."

While Kenneth spoke, Emily came up with a plan. She decided to act like she needed to go to the room to use the bathroom. Then she planned to get under the covers and fall asleep before Austin came up. Austin had already formulated the reverse plan, but he refused to leave Emily alone with Kenneth. Kenneth wished they both would go away so he could skinny dip in the cool motel pool.

According to schedule, Emily excused herself, and according to Kenneth's schedule, he waited for the motel room door to close, stood up in front of Austin and began to disrobe until the tall white bird-like man stood naked and glorious.

Kenneth then said, "Are you stupid, Austin McAdoo?"

"I beg your pardon. You're the naked one."

"Emily, man, Emily. She didn't go up to the room to use the bathroom, you goofball. She's waitin' for you. She's hot for you. Probably sittin' up there right now in one of those little black lace things, and you're down here watchin' me swim naked."

With that, Kenneth dove elegantly into the crystal pool, the water sparkling in the moonlight. Austin was scared to leave, and scared to stay, but he couldn't endure more of Kenneth's sex talk, so he stood and walked up the steps to the room on the second floor. Austin hesitated at the door and looked down at the pool, but he couldn't see Kenneth in the darkness. A voice rose up from below. "Hey, throw me down a bar of soap, would you?"

Austin pictured the man washing himself in the pool like it was his own private bathtub.

Inside, Austin was both relieved and disappointed at seeing Emily curled up in her bed, eyes closed. He was scared, but at the same time he was a man, and the internal animal instinct to spread the seed was strong and stubborn, capable of outlasting fear or trepidation, and kept Austin awake playing games with his overactive imagination. And then the snoring began.

As before, it started as a wheeze. The wheeze progressed to a cute snort. And then the snort exploded in size and volume until the room was filled with the vibrations of a small water buffalo.

The phone rang. Austin grabbed it quickly.

"Hello," he said.

"Mr. McAdoo, this is Victor at the desk. We've received a noise complaint. I thought maybe you'd left your television on when you fell asleep."

The background noise made it difficult for Austin to hear what the man said.

"There's nothing wrong with my television," he growled. As Austin struggled to listen, he watched Glenn hop down from Emily's bed and walk casually into the light from the bathroom. Austin's suitcase was on the floor, open, next to the bathroom sink. Amazed, Austin watched Glenn step into the suitcase, squat, and piss a thin stream into his folded clothes.

"Ahh," Austin yelled out.

Emily jumped up.

The man on the phone said, "What's the matter, Mr. McAdoo?"

Austin yelled, "There's nothing wrong with our TV," and slammed the phone down. He set his sights on the demon cat.

Glenn, nobody's fool, took a beeline under Emily's bed, careful to select a place with numerous exit choices.

"What's the matter?" Emily asked sleepily.

"Glenn, the cat, Beelzebub, lord of the flies, has chosen my open suitcase to do his business. Cat urine ranks ahead of toxic waste in almost every category."

"Who was that on the telephone?" she asked.

"Victor, the man at the front desk, he wanted to know if there was something wrong with our television."

"Is there?"

"No, there isn't."

Emily pondered. "That's weird."

Austin said, "Yes, it's weird. It's all weird. There's a naked man bathing in the swimming pool downstairs. There's a cat using my suitcase for a toilet. And I haven't slept all night."

Before Austin could finish his rant, Emily fell peacefully back to sleep. Austin looked at her a few minutes. He stretched the telephone line into the bathroom, closed the door, sat on the commode, and called his mother. He knew she'd be awake at 2:30.

"Mom."

"Austin? What's the matter? Is this one of those late-night phone calls a mother dreads? You're in jail, or maybe lost in the desert, or you've gotten some pesky venereal disease and need me to wire money to a Mexican clinic."

There was silence on the line. No quick come back. No sigh of exasperation. Lila McAdoo recognized the silence.

"Sorry," she said.

Austin started, "You told me my father was buried in Las Vegas. I assumed it was Las Vegas, Nevada. On the map there's a Las Vegas, New Mexico. Before I drive a thousand more miles, I thought I'd make sure which one it is."

There was silence again. "You're serious, aren't you?"

"Yes, Mother, I am."

"Don't be too serious, Austin. It's not good. Hold on a minute."

Lila pulled the old cardboard box from the closet. She shuffled through papers, photographs, and newspaper clippings until she found what she was looking for.

"Well, it's a good thing you called. The crazy old bastard is buried in Pinewood Grove Cemetery in Las Vegas, New Mexico."

Austin reduced the information to memory. Outside the bathroom door, the snore began to rise again.

"Honey," Lila said, "don't expect too much."

For no apparent reason, Austin felt emotion rise up inside him. The idea of his father had taken many shapes. As a boy he would spend hours upon hours wondering.

"It's all about expectations, honey," Lila said.

"That's exactly what the chicken man said, Mom. It's all about expectations. Is it best to have none at all? Is it best to refuse to plan for an uncertain future like little Kenny Mint?"

Lila reached for the pack of cigarettes. "Little Kenny Mint? I remember that kid. I thought he was dead."

"Oh, he's not dead. He's alive and well, bathing nude downstairs in the motel pool. He lives in the backseat of my car, along with two cats and a coat made of human hair."

Lila McAdoo laughed. "Are you on peyote?"

Austin heard the flick of the cigarette lighter.

"Mother, you told me you were going to stop smoking."

"That was twenty years ago, Austin. I said it one time in a moment of weakness and you've mentioned it three or four thousand times since then. I will not quit smoking. Now, you go to sleep, wake up tomorrow when the peyote wears off, drive to Las Vegas, New Mexico, with your girlfriend and see your father's grave. Get it behind you, move along, and call me when something good happens. I love you."

After he hung up, Austin sat in the bathroom a long time.

The next day, before they left the state of Texas, Emily bought a souvenir snow shaker. Inside, two long-horned steers stood with white flakes of synthetic snow falling and gathering at their hooves.

Austin stopped at a gas station outside of Las Vegas, New Mexico and asked for directions to the Pinewood Grove Cemetery. Kenneth was asleep in the back when they drove through the wrought-iron entrance. Austin went inside the tiny office and found an ancient woman sitting at a desk.

"I would like a map of graves so I can locate one particular person."

The old lady was wrinkled and suspicious. "Who might that be, young man?"

"It doesn't concern you. Map, please?" he said, and stuck out his enormous hand.

The lady stared at Austin long and hard with her beady blue eyes. Finally she said, "I don't like you young man. I don't like you at all."

The standoff continued. After a full minute, the old wrinkled lady handed over the map.

They drove through the cemetery around the snakelike, one-lane paved road and stopped near the back corner. Austin studied the map, and Emily stayed quiet. She waited to see if he would ask her to walk with him.

"O.K.," Austin said, "it's about a hundred yards over by the fence."

He climbed out of the car. Emily sat still. Austin walked around to the passenger side and opened her door. Emily tried not to smile. They held hands and walked slowly through the graveyard. Some of the headstones had flowers and other items around their bases. Emily wondered who put them there. Wives, lonely mothers, children, people who love the people buried beneath the ground in fancy caskets. People who watched them die, or got calls in the middle of the night, or prayed unanswered prayers alone at hospitals. People who themselves would be buried in the earth and have others, hopefully, lay flowers and notes at the base of a headstone on a Sunday after church.

Austin stopped and looked at the map one more time. He pointed to a headstone standing alone to the left next to a chain-link fence. He took a big deep breath and walked slowly with Emily by his side to his father's grave.

They both stood quietly, the heat from the sun ever-present. The silence was heavy.

On the engraved gray marble headstone were the words:

LUCUS FONTANA McADOO

BORN 1945 - DIED 1988

"LOVIN' MUSTARD MAN"

Minutes passed. Kenneth Mint appeared behind them holding Ulysses. He squinted in the bright sunlight to read the words.

"What does that mean?" he asked.

"I don't know," Austin answered. "I don't know what it means," he repeated. "Does it say 'Lovin' Mustard Man'?"

Instead of flowers at the base of the headstone, there was a blank white envelope. Reverently, Emily walked around the place the body would be buried and picked up the envelope. She gave it to Austin, who was standing in the same place.

The envelope was sealed, slightly weathered, and had a stamp in the right-hand corner. Austin opened it.

On a small piece of white paper, written in blue ink, were the words:

"Don't make the same mistakes I made."

Emily and Kenneth leaned in from opposite sides to read the note.

"What does that mean?" Kenneth asked.

Austin turned on him. "I don't know. I don't know what any of it means. Why would anyone put 'Lovin' Mustard Man' as the summation of their life?

"If it's all right with you, I'd very much like to get in the car and drive to the Grand Canyon. Is that O.K. with you? Is it?" he demanded.

Kenneth stepped back. He took one last look at the headstone.

"It's O.K. with me," Kenneth said. "I've been wantin' to go to the Grand Canyon all my life."

CHAPTER 7

It started to rain. Since the unfortunate encounter with the rock, Austin had been unable to see very well in the rearview mirror through the cracked glass of the back window. The wipers pushed the wet dust to the side and left streaks of yellow-brown on the front windshield.

Austin was weary of thinking about his father's headstone message and the mysterious note. He set out on a diatribe.

"The world's population teeters on the balance. Forty-nine percent are drug addicts, prostitutes, liars, tricksters, schizophrenics, and hooligans. The other fifty-one percent are not. It's just a matter of time before the balance tips in their favor. And then what?

"They can outvote us. Granted, many of these malcontents aren't registered voters, but they will be. Pornography will become mandatory. Prescription medication will be added to food products so we stay stoned all day long. Who will pay taxes?"

The final question hung inside the stuffy car.

"Turn on the air conditioner," Kenneth begged.

"I've told you," Austin said, "the air conditioner is out of Freon."

Kenneth asked, "Is the radio out of Freon?"

Emily tried to turn on the radio for the fifteenth time.

"It doesn't work," she said again, "but we don't need it."

Since leaving the cemetery, Emily had sensed Austin's mood change. She'd never been in love before, but she believed love was one hundred percent. It wasn't just fifty-fifty. Each person had to be prepared every minute to cover the entire one hundred percent when the other person couldn't carry their share of the load.

Emily reached her hand across the console and let it rest on Austin's thigh. Kenneth saw the gesture. Hunched down in the backseat, with Glenn napping on his chest, Kenneth said, "You know what I think? I think love has a life span. You know, like a mosquito only lives a certain number of days. Love has an incubation period, a life span, and that's it. Afterwards, it's just two people trying to get along, mimicking love, like actors in a Broadway play. But you can't keep it alive, it's like pounding the chest of a dead body, it just won't breathe."

The rain fell harder. Emily's forehead wrinkled in

thought. She said to Kenneth, "You're like the tin man in *The Wizard of Oz.* You don't have a heart."

Glenn raised his head, looked slowly around the cramped car, and settled back to sleep.

Kenneth asked, "I forget, what were the other two missing? The scarecrow and the big lion?"

Emily answered, "The scarecrow was missing a brain, and the lion was missing courage."

Kenneth asked, "Did they have a red car and two cats on the way to California?"

Emily shook her head, "No, stupid. They walked on the yellow brick road and had a little dog named Toto on the way to the land of Oz."

Glenn yawned.

A loud, knocking sound came from the engine. The car began to decelerate in the rain.

"What was that?" Emily asked.

"Big trouble," Austin answered. The internal workings of an automobile held the same mystery to Austin McAdoo as outer space. He knew what holes to put gasoline and oil. After that, it was all elliptical. Austin felt fear at the prospect of being stationary.

The car came to rest on the side of Interstate 40 outside of Bluewater, New Mexico. Just a few seconds earlier they had all been flying across the surface of the planet at seventy-one miles per hour. Now, with the windows rolled up, they sat listening to cars and trucks whizzing past on the wet highway.

Emily said, "Maybe it'll start working in a few minutes."

Kenneth responded, "It must be interesting to believe things like that."

Luckily, inertia led the vehicle to a stop only yards from the exit ramp. Kenneth sat up in his seat, disturbing Glenn. He rubbed a spot on the window and peered outside in the mist at a sign for Winslow's Automotive Repair.

"I guess we're pushin'," he said.

Emily climbed in the driver's seat after the men got out of the car. She did as Kenneth said and put the car in neutral after turning the key to unlock the steering wheel. Austin had seen a video clip on television depicting a truck losing control on a wet roadway and slamming into a police car on the side of the road. He pushed the car with half-strength, his eyes over his shoulder.

"Put your weight behind it, big boy," Kenneth said. And when Austin did, the car picked up speed, reached the top of the incline, and headed down the hill of the exit ramp, leaving the two men standing behind in the drizzling rain. They walked. The butt whistle sang twice before they reached the garage. The rain stopped.

The mechanic, Billy Winslow, only had one normal arm. The other arm never grew properly in the womb and was the size of a G.I. Joe arm, perfectly formed, but useless. Billy kept it covered to protect the small fingers and avoid the stares. Sometimes, at home, alone, he would pay attention to the appendage, but never at the garage.

After the initial introductions, Kenneth took Billy off to the side.

"You seem like a good guy. Got your own place here. Overcome a disability."

Kenneth faked hesitation. "I shouldn't be telling you this. We're with a TV news show. That big fella is the producer. The girl is an actress. We travel around the country and catch mechanics overcharging folks for car repair. They've got eleven tiny hidden cameras in the engine."

Billy Winslow listened. "You wouldn't believe how many times we've busted guys replacin' parts that don't need replacin' or chargin' for work they hadn't even done."

Kenneth glanced over his shoulder, pretending to be secretive.

"Now, I know you wouldn't do nothin' like that, but I just thought you might be extra careful. One old boy we got in Oklahoma just made a simple mistake, but by the time it got on television, hell, he done lost his shop, his license, everything."

Billy rubbed his good hand on his pants leg.

"And by the way, Billy, why don't you go ahead and fix the A/C and the radio. The actress has plenty of money."

Kenneth winked and held up his thumb. Billy Winslow didn't know what to think about the things Kenneth said, so he didn't think about them at all. He just did what he did, fix cars.

•

The sun began to shine. Austin found the pay phone and called his mother.

"Hello."

"Mother, I went to the cemetery and found Dad's grave. It says 'Lovin' Mustard Man'. What does that mean? What could that possibly mean?"

Lila laughed hard. She began to cough midway through the laugh until she was coughing like a smoker. Austin held the phone away from his ear. When the cough ended, Lila laughed again.

"I'd like to know what's so funny? Is it some type of code? Is it a message only certain people understand?"

Lila smiled. "It's no code. It's just what it says. The man loved mustard. He loved it. Everybody's got to have something."

Austin stood soaking wet in the new sunshine. He felt the heat begin to rise from the pavement. He said, "That's the best he could do? That's what he puts on his gravestone, 'Lovin' Mustard Man'? I don't believe it. I just don't believe it."

Lila said, "That's all right. You don't have to believe it. You can believe whatever you want, Austin, but who's to say mustard is less important than anything else? When you find what's important to you in this world, it becomes part of you. Life is messy, boy. You've got to get your hands dirty. Get down in it."

She coughed again.

"I found a note on his grave. A little note inside an envelope. It wasn't addressed to anybody. It said, 'Don't make the same mistakes I made.'"

Lila caught her breath on the backside of the last cough.

"That's horseshit, Austin. The mistakes are the best part. If you took all the perfect moments in your life and strung them together, the movie would last about fifteen minutes, and everybody in the theater would be bored out of their gourds."

Austin raised his voice. "I don't even know why I call you."

"I'm your mother, Austin. I'm your mother. That's why you call me. You climbed out of my vagina. We were connected by a cord. You sucked at my breast. That's why you chose to call me instead of a random person in the phonebook. And besides that, you know I'm right.

"You need to get laid, Austin. You need to get laid, and you need to float in the Pacific Ocean, and you need to stretch out in the desert all night with Emily under the stars."

Austin watched Emily walk across the street to a small store. She practically skipped.

"I shot fireworks, Mom."

"What?"

"I shot fireworks."

"It's about time. Maybe everything will be O.K. after all, Honey. Now let me go. I've got cigarettes to smoke."

Winslow's Automotive Repair sat next to the Bluewater Little League Baseball Park. Since the beginning of Kenneth Mint's memory, baseball had been a part of his life. Through the upheaval, baseball remained, steady, unchanging, dependable, waiting patiently from the last pitch of the World Series to the first pitch of spring.

Austin took off his wet shirt and put on a fresh one from his suitcase. Unfortunately, it wasn't so fresh. Cat urine surrounded Austin McAdoo like an invisible cloud of radiation.

They all three sat at a wooden picnic table down the third-base line of the field. A canned ham was opened for the occasion, and Emily delivered three cold Coca-Colas.

"I've got another souvenir to go with the long-horns," Emily announced.

It was a miniature pueblo, brown, made of sand from the desert. At the base, in red letters, it said, 'New Mexico.'

"One day, when I'm older, I'll have all the souvenirs from this trip on a glass shelf in my living room. I can look at them anytime I want and remember all the stuff we did."

"You ever play wiffle ball?" Kenneth asked.

Emily sipped her cold Coke. "No, what's that?"

"It's like baseball, only the ball has holes on one side. You can make it dance. We played every day when I was a kid. We kept stats. There's a notebook somewhere in this world with wins and losses, home runs, errors, all of it. You ever play wiffle ball, Austin?"

He knew the game. He remembered, as a young boy, sitting at the window watching the kids from the neighborhood play in Brandon Crawford's yard across the street. He remembered sitting inside the classroom during recess and watching little Kenny Mint and the others throw the white plastic ball.

"No," Austin said.

"I bet if you got hold of one, you'd send it for a ride. There's lots of big guys in baseball. Babe Ruth was a big guy. Greg Luzinski."

Kenneth stopped for a moment, looked over at the baseball field, and said, "We should play. Right now, on that field, while we wait for the car."

Austin said, "I don't believe you'll find a wiffle ball around here."

"Sure I will," Kenneth answered. "I've got one in my bag."

Fifteen minutes later they stood in the dirt at home plate.

"Where'd you get this bat?" Austin asked.

"Don't worry about that," Kenneth replied.

It was a yellow plastic bat. Emily gripped it and took a few swings in the air. Her form was poor, but the enthusiasm more than compensated. Kenneth tried not to look at the miniskirt.

Kenneth was like a kid again. "I used to throw a wicked little curve ball. It came in at the batter, twelve o'clock, and dropped to six o'clock by the time it crossed the plate. I'll pitch."

Emily batted first. Kenneth's arm was rusty, and his pitches sailed. Emily swung like she couldn't wait but never touched the ball. After he warmed up, Kenneth's pitches began to work as he'd remembered. The outside fastball set up the curve. The change-up made the fastball seem unhittable.

Austin McAdoo became quite nervous. In his mind, so many years ago, Austin imagined the day he would play with the other kids. The miraculous catch at the centerfield wall to steal a home run. The overpowering fastball he would use to strike out Brandon Crawford. Mostly, he envisioned the towering home run he'd crack into Mrs. Renfroe's bushes to win the game amid clapping and cheers.

"Your turn, Austin," Emily said, and held out the yellow bat.

He hesitated. Austin looked at Emily, and she looked back at him.

Austin took the bat. He stepped into the box at home plate and dug his shoes into the dirt the way Brandon Crawford used to do. He looked out over the green grass of the field.

Kenneth Mint decided to start with his famous curve ball. He gripped the ball, holes to the outside, and stared at his target. Austin's knees were weak. He held the bat in his huge hands, lifting the barrel off his shoulder.

Emily sensed a rise in testosterone. She didn't

understand it completely, but her instincts told her the silly game somehow meant more than it should.

"Are you ready, big boy?" Kenneth taunted.

Austin tightened. His eyes thinned to slits, and he ignored the smell of cat pee about his person.

Kenneth wound up, kicked his leg, and came over the top with a perfect curve ball, tumbling toward the plate at a high rate of speed. With only a split-second to react, Austin McAdoo unleashed a mighty swing with the yellow plastic bat. Every ounce of strength, every pound of flesh, came together in one exhilarating moment.

There was the sound of the plastic bat nicking the plastic ball, and the ball veered off the bat to the backstop. A foul ball. Not a majestic home run. Not an embarrassing strike. A foul ball. A victory of sorts for Austin McAdoo, but there were no cheers or clapping, only the sight of a one-armed mechanic standing behind the backstop where the ball came to rest.

Billy Winslow said, "Your car's fixed."

Austin was relieved. He would embrace the small victory and move along.

Emily yelled, "Grand Canyon here we come."

Kenneth Mint found a comfortable spot amongst the debris in the backseat. He smiled widely and said, "You know, sometimes when mechanics fix one part of a car, other parts begin to magically work again. Let's all pray for the air-conditioning and the radio to be restored." Kenneth bowed his head, chin to chest.

"Lord, please hear our prayer. We have traveled long and far in the heat and silence. Lift your almighty hand and touch us with your grace and love. Fix our A/C so we might feel the coolness on our hot faces. Fix the radio so we can hear the joy of music in our ears. Amen."

Kenneth lifted his head to see Emily and Austin staring back at him.

"Try it," he said.

They continued to stare. Emily said, "You really shouldn't bother God with little stuff. You should save it until you need somethin' big. He's busy."

"Not today," Kenneth responded. "Today, he's got time to help us out. God helps those who help themselves. It says so in the Bible. Now try it."

Emily turned the knob. A cool blast of arctic air blew through her hair. She was stunned and swung around to see Kenneth Mint with his curious smile.

"Try the radio."

Emily turned the radio knob. Static filled the car. She pressed a button and they heard Mick Jagger's throaty voice sing words undetermined.

"Roll up the windows," Kenneth demanded, "and wake me when we arrive at our destination. For it is not the path one takes, nor the place one arrives, that matters most. Instead, it is the comfort in which we travel and our relationship with God during the journey that matters most. Mark my words, the devil don't like roast beef."

With that, Kenneth snuggled between the hair coat and Ulysses, his left ear purposefully left unobstructed.

Emily looked at Austin and mouthed the words, "Roast beef."

Austin thought she said, "horse teeth," and shook his bowling-ball head in misunderstanding.

"What?" he whispered.

"Roast beef?" she whispered back.

Kenneth said, "I heard that. The devil don't like roast beef."

Emily turned up the radio a notch and waited until she could hear Kenneth's breathing deepen. She dared to swivel her head slowly around to look in the backseat. On Kenneth's cheek was a small red ant. Emily watched the ant casually move around the cheek, stop at the edge of the lip, and then work its way up near the steep incline of the bridge of the nose.

Forgetting her plan to allow Kenneth Mint to drift away to sleep, Emily whispered through the music, "There's a little ant on you."

Without opening his eyes, Kenneth said, "I'm aware."

Emily watched the tiny creature ascend the slope of the nose, ease down the incline on the other side, and nonchalantly stroll near the orbit of the eye socket.

Eyes still closed, Kenneth said, "He lives on me. Everything has to live somewhere, and this ant lives on me. Don't worry, he finds plenty to eat."

Emily thought about the ant, foraging for bits of

dry dead skin on the landscape of Kenneth Mint like a tiny cow. She watched a moment longer and then turned to face forward, content to resort to the original plan of allowing the strange man in the backseat to fall asleep.

Austin planned to take Interstate 40 west from Bluewater into Arizona approximately two hundred and eighty miles to Highway 64. From there it would be a straight shot north to the Grand Canyon. He calculated they would arrive shortly before nightfall. Those calculations were based upon an average speed of seventy-one miles per hour with a single forty-five minute rest stop, clear weather, no construction delays, and Austin's ability to tolerate the intolerable smell of his clothing inside the sealed vehicle.

"I'm so proud of you," Emily said. "Hitting that ball like you did. I tried, but I couldn't hit it."

Unconsciously, Austin's chest stuck out just a little. Yes, it was no towering home run, but on his first official swing ever he fouled off little Kenny Mint's famous curve ball. And more importantly, someone else grasped the importance.

"Thank you," he said proudly.

They were quiet a moment. Emily's soft hand slid once again to Austin's leg and rested against his thigh. Austin swallowed and then calmly moved his right hand from the leather steering wheel, covering Emily's hand completely. It was comfortable and exhilarating at the same time.

Emily said softly, "When I first saw you that night

in the club, I knew you were the one. Some people don't believe in that, fate and all, but I know it's for real."

Austin couldn't decide what to say. He wanted to tell Emily he loved her. He wanted to tell her nothing meant anything until the night she got in his car. But he couldn't speak the words. Something inside Austin McAdoo, the holy instinct of self-protection, wouldn't let him climb boldly out onto the limb of life. He'd done it before, as a child, and suffered the ridicule of a fat pilgrim. He'd heard the smirks too many times, seen the smiles of the pretty girls behind his back. So Emily said it for him.

"I love you," she said, looking down at her knees.

Austin felt a flush rise slowly from the middle of his massive chest. It was the same flush he felt in the fireworks stand moments before he'd fainted and crushed the table.

Austin hyperventilated, "Take the wheel. Take the wheel, I say."

So she did.

Austin listened to Rod Stewart's rendition of "*Have I Told You Lately That I Love You*" on the radio. For a brief period he had no idea where he was and felt physically like a man resting on a cloud. He was weak, and in his weakness remembered Emily's words.

In the hours that followed, Kenneth slept soundly. Emily drifted off to sleep herself, and Austin thought. He felt, for the first time in his life, a quiet serenity, and inside the cocoon of this serenity, Austin began to imagine the possibilities.

He felt as if he had been concealed within his body, and now, at least temporarily, as if he was no longer concealed. No longer that fat kid, or the smart-ass giant, or the cowardly lion. Now he was the 'one.' He was somebody's fate. And that somebody, Emily Dooley, embraced the fate like she was the luckiest of God's children. Almost as lucky as Austin himself.

They traveled Highway 64. Everyone was awake, and each felt the excitement of anticipation. The sign said GRAND CANYON NATIONAL PARK — 40 miles, and then 20 miles, and then they were there.

Austin parked the car, and the three walked together to a scenic overlook. The sun was setting in the west, a red-orange painted backdrop.

They stood at the edge and looked down. Pictures in books or postcards from relatives had not done the canyon justice. Words in brochures were insufficient. The Grand Canyon was vast and glorious. The three travelers stood side by side, speechless, their senses filled to the brink.

Austin McAdoo was overcome. He felt an upsurge of emotion standing next to Emily. There was no plan. There was no practicing the words. The enormity of the place and situation, standing on the precipice, dictated events.

Austin McAdoo fell to his knee, held Emily's tiny hand in his palm, and said, "Will you marry me, Emily

Dooley?"

Thereafter came a moment. He hadn't foreseen saying anything at all, much less proposing marriage.

Kenneth was dumbstruck at the raw courage, and a bit jealous of the possibilities.

Emily had lived the moment a thousand times, different places, different dresses, usually with a sunset, and often overlooking the Grand Canyon. She looked down at her future husband and felt the tears rise and gently release from her unwavering eyes. She smiled the way a woman can smile at such times, and Austin waited on bended knee.

"Yes, Austin, I will marry you," she said, as the last slice of the sun melted on the horizon.

Austin McAdoo fainted on cue. His great weight fell against the unsteady railing. For a brief instant, Kenneth felt sure he was about to see Austin's body break through the barrier and tumble helplessly into the great canyon below.

But the barrier held, and Austin merely crumbled to the cement, rolling with the assistance of Emily and Kenneth into a prone position, and then awakening quickly with the sensation of a dream.

But it was no dream. Austin had proposed marriage. Emily ran to get a wet paper towel from the bathroom. Kenneth leaned over the big man.

"Hey, have you lost your freakin' mind? Tell her you were delirious. Tell her you forgot your vitamin. It doesn't count if you weren't lucid."

Austin said, "I don't take vitamins."

"Well, maybe you should."

Emily arrived out of breath. She dabbed the wet towel on Austin's wooden forehead.

"We need to find a place to spend the night," she said. "Get you in a cool room."

They found a cottage just down the road. Kenneth sat on the porch sipping water from a glass and feeling left out. He wasn't sure he'd completely understood what he'd seen. He felt the ant move across his scalp. Kenneth resisted the urge to scratch.

Austin and Emily washed up and changed clothes. They joined Kenneth on the porch.

"Well, when's the big day?" Kenneth asked.

"We were going to talk to you about that," Emily said. "We were hopin', you being a preacher and all, that you might marry us in Los Angeles. I always wanted to get married down there on Hollywood Boulevard."

Kenneth looked out across the landscape. He took a sip of his water and put the glass down on the table. The time had come. The soft underbelly had presented itself.

"Well, I'll do that for you, under one condition."

"What's that?" Austin said skeptically.

"No man should get married, at least not the first time, without a proper bachelor party. I'll marry you. Yes I will. But first we've got to stay tomorrow night in Las Vegas, the real Las Vegas, so I can take Mr. McAdoo out on the town one last time."

Both Austin and Emily were uncomfortable with

the idea, but neither mustered an objection.

"It's tradition," Kenneth said.

Austin went inside to look at the new map. He needed to see the route in his mind.

Kenneth and Emily were left alone on the porch.

Kenneth said, "I hate to ask you, but I'm a little low on money these days. Austin deserves a bachelor party, a nice one, just like you deserve a nice wedding dress. I know a place in Los Angeles, owned by a guy named Angelo, where we can get you a pretty white dress like you've always imagined."

Emily thought about the dress. She could see it. She could see herself in the full-length mirror with her hands folded in front. She jotted down the name "Angelo" on a piece of paper.

"Now a good bachelor party usually runs around two thousand dollars, but I can cut a few corners and do it up right for maybe a thousand. Maybe," Kenneth added.

Emily had counted her money after she paid the mechanic in Bluewater. It didn't seem fair to spend it all on herself. She could sleep in the car in Las Vegas if she had to. Austin deserved a bachelor party.

"O.K.," she said. "As long as he doesn't touch any girls. He can look, but he just can't touch."

Kenneth smiled. "You drive a hard bargain, young lady, but that's a deal."

In his mind, Kenneth could see the money. Crisp new one hundred dollar bills. Ten of them. A nice neat stack. Emily could see the dress, white, flowing, beautiful against her skin. The dress she saw in a magazine so many years ago. And Austin, big Austin, laying across the bed on his stomach studying the map of the western United States, could see clearly the route he would take to Las Vegas, Nevada, the city of sin.

CHAPTER 8

The sun rose the next morning on the other side of the canyon wall. Kenneth watched it come up, inch by inch, as he stared directly into the orange ball. For no particular reason, he thought about the pitch he threw Austin. He questioned the choice to start off with a curve. It would have been better to blow a fastball past the rookie and set up the yellowhammer curve. But what did it matter, he thought? Who really gives a shit about a foul-tipped wiffle ball in Bluewater, New Mexico?

They stuck around for breakfast. Las Vegas was about three hundred miles away, and Emily was in no hurry to get there. She barely slept all night, replaying the marriage proposal over and over again. Envisioning her bridal gown and creating the nervousness she would feel during the ceremony as they neared the point of 'I do' forever. 'I do' now and always. 'I do,' I promise, no matter what, or why, or how many times, so help me God, I'm the gingerbread man.

They sat in the diner, Austin and Emily on one side of the booth together, Kenneth on the other sipping his black coffee. Austin ordered a large stack of buckwheat pancakes from the middle-aged Hispanic waitress. Her skin was the color of syrup.

Kenneth watched the woman closely, and when she walked away he said, "God chose to make the spectrum of a rainbow the same in every rainbow. Red, then orange, then yellow, green, blue, indigo, and violet. But he chose to make the colors of his children a completely different spectrum.

"At one end we have the whitest person in the world. Paper white. Nearly translucent. At the other end of the room we have the blackest person in the world, as dark as midnight without a moon.

"In the middle, starting at the white end, we have increasing shades of pale, pale to khaki, khaki to light brown, light brown to coffee, and so on. In between we have various shades of Asian yellow, subtle Indian red, and odd turquoise."

Kenneth stopped, took another sip of his coffee, and continued, "Why is it white dogs don't look down upon black dogs? Why is it dogs don't run in packs consisting only of their own shade? Is it natural to set ourselves apart based on these subtle differences in skin color? It's not like some of us are orange and others are violet. If that were the case, I could certainly see how the orange people might hate the violet people, and vice-versa. The juxtaposition is too extreme to ignore.

"But in the history of mankind, a constant factor throughout civilization has been the inclination to judge, sort out, simplify, and attempt to categorize people by the degree of pigmentation in their skin. Why not eye color instead of skin color? Or foot size? That would be good. People with little feet move to the front of the line. How about the shape of their ears? Round ears, you're a king. Elongated, crawl on your hands and knees for a scrap of bread."

Austin listened to the ramblings of Kenneth Mint and wondered if he felt the same way other people felt all those years listening to himself ramble. Certainly not. Before Emily, Austin McAdoo would have engaged in a spirited debate with the man across the table. Instead, he half listened and longed for his buckwheat pancakes to arrive hot off the griddle.

"I disagree," Austin stated, as the lady set his pancakes in front of him.

Emily said, "Dogs are color-blind."

"Maybe that explains it," Kenneth retorted.

Austin felt relief when the little red car started. Like a big bird, Kenneth began to make a nest in the backseat.

Emily asked, "Why do you sleep all day?"

"Because I stay awake all night."

"You don't sleep at night?"

"No, I never have. I stay awake like a bat. I don't

even try to sleep anymore when it's dark. There's no point. I used to think something was wrong with me, but now I know it's the other way around."

Kenneth waited for Emily to ask for an explanation, but instead, she pulled the laminated postcard of the Grand Canyon from her purse and held it in her lap. So Kenneth explained anyway.

"You see, predatory animals primarily hunt at night. You two would be the first to be eaten. I would survive. I've been selected to occupy the tip-top of the food chain."

Austin started to respond to Kenneth's inflammatory remark, but Emily said, "I don't think you'd taste very good. You don't eat right."

Kenneth completed his nest. Before he closed his eyes and headed for slumber, Kenneth said, "You ever see a tree die of old age?"

Austin rolled his eyes and shook his head. Ulysses crawled up into the seat with Emily, and Glenn found a spot in the hollow beneath Kenneth's flat belly.

They rode in silence for miles. Emily thought about lots of things, but finally her mind came to rest on one subject.

She asked Austin, "Have you ever been to a bachelor party before?"

"Once," he said. "My cousin Peter got married. There was a bachelor party, but I don't think my evening with batman will be much like Peter's bachelor party."

Emily hesitated and then said, "It's O.K. if you

go see girls dance, because I know that don't mean nothin'. But I don't think you should touch one, being so close to our wedding night and everything."

"I have no intention of touching anyone," he replied.

Emily smiled. "Can you promise me?" she asked.

Austin was still amazed at the young woman's degree of commitment. At times he almost believed it was a big trick and at the end he'd find himself standing alone at the altar in front of a room full of laughing strangers, the star of a new practical joke television show.

"I promise," he mumbled.

"On a stack of Bibles?" she asked.

"On a stack of Bibles," he repeated.

They drove slowly down the Las Vegas strip. None of the three had ever been to such a place. It was impressive, almost a manmade Grand Canyon, a testament to what the human mind can conceive and create in the middle of a desert. There was a suggestion of decadence. More than a suggestion. A shout. Like the hand of the devil swinging open the doors to every temptation.

Kenneth said, "All the hotels are inexpensive. They expect you to go downstairs and drop a bundle in the casino."

With Kenneth's guidance they selected a place to stay. The tall building was made of mirrors, solid, like one of those full-length dressing mirrors in the changing room at the mall, except forty stories in the sky. The bottom floor was a huge casino with slot machines, blackjack tables, and roulette wheels. It was just like on television.

Emily paid for the room, and they went upstairs to inspect it. The bed covers were maroon. Austin pulled the blinds to reveal a view down the strip. It seemed worlds away from the Grand Canyon the day before, but in America it was only three hundred miles. Three hundred miles from one extreme to another, like a crazy man.

Austin excused himself to the bathroom after Emily finished her tour.

"O.K., Emily, here's the plan. I'll take the groom for a few cocktails, maybe a big T-bone steak, check out a few casinos. We'll come back to the room around ten. You stay gone for two hours. We'll do guy stuff in the room, maybe a wholesome little show, and then I'm sure the old boy will be ready to hit the hay. So you can come back around midnight, and then I'll go hang around the car."

Emily pointed her finger up at Kenneth. "No touching. That's the rule."

Kenneth raised his hands in surrender. "That's the rule. Cross my heart. Now I need a few dollars to make Austin's last night of freedom truly memorable."

Emily had already pre-counted one thousand dollars. It was mostly five and twenty dollar bills so the wad was fat and bound in a rubber band. Kenneth put the money in his small bag and put the bag in the bottom drawer of the nightstand.

Austin exited the bathroom, still in the process of arranging his pants.

"All right, get ready to go, big boy. You're mine from now to midnight. At midnight, you turn into a pumpkin and your future wife can have you back. Until then, buckle up Austin McAdoo."

Austin felt a healthy amount of anxiety. Las Vegas, Kenneth Mint, the potential for disaster was unlimited. However, on the other side of the coin, he felt the gentle touch of the devil's hand upon his shoulder. What could be the harm? It's tradition.

Emily put her clothes in all the drawers while Austin got dressed. She turned up the air-conditioning as high as it would go and turned down the sheets. Kenneth got his bag and headed for the door. Emily was quick to reach for Austin's hand.

"You have a good time," she whispered, "and I'll see you at midnight."

She pulled the tall man down and kissed him gently on the cheek.

Austin's anxiety level increased.

"Maybe this isn't such a good idea," he said to Kenneth, who was already half out the door.

"Don't be stupid. You've got the rest of your life to feel guilty, and believe me, you will. How does a steak sound, a big T-bone? Red meat."

Austin looked back at Emily, wishing for approval. She granted his wish. "Go," she said, but it wasn't until he saw her smile that Austin felt released.

When the door closed, Emily stripped naked where she stood and crawled between the icy cool sheets.

Kenneth and Austin sat at the casino bar. "I'll have Jack Daniel's on the rocks. What do you want, Austin?" Kenneth said in front of the bartender.

"I'll have a milk punch."

"A what?" Kenneth demanded.

"A milk punch. They're very refreshing."

"This ain't the beach. Refreshing? This is a bachelor night. Bring him a whiskey like mine, except put a little Coke in it on the first few rounds to ease the burn. Start a tab."

"Where did you get money?" Austin asked.

"I put away a few dollars for a rainy day. Don't worry about it."

Austin said, "I'm sure you're quite aware I don't believe you've put away anything for a rainy day, particularly money. If you've stolen the money from Emily, I'll call the police, and you can sit in jail with your hair coat."

"I didn't steal anything. Emily wanted you to have a good time. She gave me the money."

Austin almost regretted his accusation. "How much?"

"Two hundred dollars. Enough to get drunk and have a dirty conversation with a ten-dollar hooker."

The bartender put drinks in front of the men. And then a few minutes later he put more drinks in front of the men. And then more. Austin forgot he was hungry.

Kenneth said, "We're both pariahs, outcasts. You know that, don't you? You're a smart guy. Of course, it's for different reasons. You, for physical reasons, and me for mental. Both of us pushed aside by society. Told to stand on the other side of the barricade while the stream of American society runs past like a river.

"You see, you don't look like those people in the magazines. And I don't think like 'em."

Austin puffed up. "I'm offended by that."

Kenneth replied, "Good. That's good. Being offended is human. Not being offended is the problem. Everybody walks around pretending to be offended, but they really aren't."

Austin said, "By the way, I've never seen anyone in a magazine who looks remotely similar to you. My proportions may be large, but you resemble a rodent."

"A rodent?" Kenneth asked.

"Yes."

"Bartender," Kenneth called, "bring us two refreshing milk punches. One for my disproportionate friend, and one for the rodent."

The bartender paid no attention to the comment and set off to make two milk punches.

"You don't really have a butt whistle, do you?"

"Do you want to see it?"

"I absolutely do not want to see it."

"Why not?"

"Obvious reasons."

Kenneth laughed. "A rodent? I like that." He laughed

again.

The casino was bustling. Fat women and flashing lights were everywhere. Austin was at the happy point of intoxication where his mind believed the joy could last indefinitely if he would only keep drinking. The milk punch seemed like candy after the third whiskey.

Austin rose from the barstool to go to the bathroom. For a moment he was unsteady on his flat feet and a bit dizzy. The dizziness passed.

When Austin was gone, Kenneth asked the bartender, "Let's say a guy was looking for a cheap hooker, maybe a little overweight, or maybe a little over the hill, to do a dance, maybe rub up against my big friend. Where would a guy go?"

The bartender didn't smile. He just pulled a pen from his pocket and wrote a name and phone number on the back of a napkin.

Kenneth picked it up and read, "Tina."

Austin returned.

Kenneth commented, "You still smell like cat piss."

"And you, Mr. Mint, have insects that live on you full-time."

"That reminds me," Kenneth said. He then took a small pretzel from the bowl on the bar, held the pretzel above his head, and snapped it in half, sending several small white pieces of crunchy material into his hair.

Austin watched. He felt no need for further explanation. Somehow, it almost seemed perfectly normal. He took another sip of his drink.

"Let's gamble a little," Kenneth suggested.

While Austin lost eight dollars in the slot machines, Kenneth called Tina.

"Hello, Tina?"

"Who's asking?"

"Well, Captain Kenneth St. John of the United States Navy. I got your name from a friend. I'm in town entertaining Senator Austin McAdoo from the fine state of Alabama. We'd like to retain your services."

Tina was silent. Then she asked, "What services did you have in mind?"

"Well now, in Alabama they'd be illegal. But here in Las Vegas, it's just a business transaction. A little dance, a little pleasure, a little money."

"How much money?"

"Five hundred."

"You got a deal, Captain John."

Kenneth told her to meet him at the hotel room at 10:15. That way, he'd be sure Emily had vacated the premises.

Another whiskey. And then the waitress brought another, no Coke added. Austin was drunk like a goat. The world was a spinning ball of lights, big-breasted waitresses, bells, and silver coins.

Kenneth carried his bag on his shoulder. At 10:05 he found Austin staring intently at a cowboy poker player wearing a black ten-gallon hat.

"Hey, Austin, let's go upstairs. Maybe we can order a little room service. I've still got a few dollars left."

Austin leaned against the wall inside the elevator,

unsteady.

"Where do you think Emily is?" he asked.

Kenneth didn't answer.

"Have you ever told anybody you loved them? It's hard. It's like standing naked," the large man said almost to himself.

Kenneth listened. Then he asked, "Do you have any friends, Austin?"

In Austin's drunken state, inhibitions dissolved, he said the first thing that drifted into his mind. "You."

The elevator door opened. Austin got off and turned in the wrong direction. Kenneth waited a moment longer and then caught the door before it closed.

Inside the room, while Austin washed his face, Kenneth counted out one hundred dollars. There was a knock at the door.

"Is that Emily?" Austin mumbled from the bathroom.

"No," Kenneth said. "It's room service. I'll take care of it."

Kenneth opened the door to see a female toad, maybe forty-five years old, short, squat, bleach-blonde hair, wearing a thin powder-blue dress. She smelled like cigarettes and carried a hideous little sequined purse, faded yellow.

"Wow," Kenneth said without thinking. "You must be Tina. Thanks for coming. Senator McAdoo is inside washing up. Here's one hundred dollars."

"You said five hundred."

"Oh, you'll get that and more. Every fifteen minutes you spend with the senator, I'll give you one hundred dollars just like this. If he likes you, you could be here all night. Now let me tell you, he's shy. He's gonna want to talk, but he likes his women to start the action, so you be the one to get it going."

"Where's your uniform?" Tina asked.

"We can't wear uniforms when we meet with prostitutes. It's against regulations. Now let me introduce you."

Austin walked out of the bathroom, drying his face with a towel. He removed the towel to see Tina the toad.

"Where's our food?" he asked.

Kenneth said, "Mr. McAdoo, this is Tina. She will bring you great pleasure. I'll go get you a snack, and I'll be back shortly."

Kenneth, his bag still around his shoulder, walked out the door. He entered the elevator alone, pressed the button, and rode alone all the way to the casino. He planned to walk out the door, take a bus to Los Angeles, and count his money on the way. But Kenneth Mint passed a roulette wheel. The silver ball rolled round and round the red and black wheel. He stopped.

He knew he had a few minutes. At least fifteen. So he bought a hundred dollars in chips and decided to let it ride on red. He set the chips down and looked up to see Emily Dooley enter the casino. She walked slowly, looking down like she was counting her steps to the elevator. Kenneth hunkered behind a large woman from Pittsburgh and watched Emily make her way to the elevator. She got inside and the doors closed.

Kenneth asked the woman from Pittsburgh, "What time is it?"

"10:30," she said.

Emily Dooley reached the right floor. She walked slowly down the hall, questioning herself. Why should she have to sit in the car? Was Austin McAdoo a man of his word? How would she know if she didn't see for herself?

She was right, and she was wrong, but mostly she was curious to the point of exhaustion.

Emily listened at the door. She heard a rustling. The sound of a pillow hitting the floor. She eased the key card into the slot, opened the door slowly, and saw a naked woman. An incredibly ugly naked woman straddling the fully-clothed torso of Austin McAdoo, her backside to Austin's face, her frontside to the door, saggy breasts and white high-heeled shoes cocked in the air.

Austin was so drunk he could barely see. He had actually fallen asleep, but unfortunately, Tina's body blocked his view of the door, and therefore, blocked Emily's view of Austin's closed eyes.

"Who are you?" Tina said. "Nobody said nothin' about a threesome."

Emily's anger was like a fire.

"You promised," she screamed. "You promised. You were supposed to be different. You swore on a stack of Bibles."

Austin opened his eyes to see the bare ass of what appeared to be an elderly woman wearing white high-heels. Before he could gather his wits, and remove the blonde rider, Emily had packed her bags and was heading out the door.

"Emily, Emily," he wailed, like a wounded animal. But it was too late. She was gone. And Austin fell to his knees in the room, unable to chase her. Unable to stop his world from crumbling to pieces before his bloodshot eyes.

Tina said, "I ain't leavin' without my extra hundred bucks. I've been here more than fifteen minutes."

Austin turned to look at the naked woman. He couldn't focus his eyes.

"Where's Captain John?" she asked.

Austin said with displeasure, "I know no one by the name of Captain John."

"Well, I ain't leavin'. Maybe I'll just call the cops. I'm sure a senator like yourself ain't too interested in causin' a big scene. Might end up in the newspapers."

Austin squeezed up his face. "Lord God, what are you talking about? Please leave me in my misery, naked woman."

"I ain't leavin'," she said. "It smells like cat pee in here."

Downstairs, Kenneth won three times in a row. He bet red, then black, then red again, skipping a turn in between each time. The elevator door opened and Emily Dooley charged out, a suitcase in each hand. Kenneth followed her to the glass door and watched her storm across the parking lot to the little red car. He watched as Emily headed toward the street, trying to balance Ulysses and Glenn without dropping a suitcase.

Kenneth Mint stood at the roulette wheel with four hundred dollars in chips. He took a deep breath and thought about things. He thought about the day his wife walked out the door with her red suitcase. He just sat there on the couch and watched her go. He stayed that way the whole day, unable to make himself get up. He didn't even turn on the television. Just sat there looking at the door, expecting her to come back any minute. But she never did. She never came back, and eventually, he had to get up off the couch and go somewhere.

He was in Las Vegas. He had one thousand two hundred dollars and a free chance to walk away. Austin McAdoo, a childhood classmate, was upstairs in a hotel room far from home with a belligerent prostitute and a shattered future. But he didn't owe Austin McAdoo anything. He didn't owe anybody anything. That was the beauty of having nothing.

Still, Kenneth Mint stared at the elevator. He was angry at his inability to walk away. He was disappointed at his failure to short-circuit the human condition. He'd spent years, dedicated a substantial portion of his recent life to disconnecting, and now, when his efforts were put to the test, he couldn't walk out.

The gold doors of the elevator opened. Austin

McAdoo emerged. He was barefoot, shirt unbuttoned, and his black wavy hair was caught in a hurricane of inebriation. Austin stumbled, regained his balance, and set off quickly across the casino in the direction of the front door. At his heels, like a barking Jack Russell, followed Tina, the bleach-blonde prostitute, with a high-heeled shoe in each hand.

As Austin increased his pace, Tina turned up the volume on purpose. "Senator McAdoo! Senator McAdoo! Why are you in such a hurry?"

Heads in the casino began to turn. Austin bumbled down the aisle of blackjack tables, all heads followed as he passed.

"Where's Captain John?" she nearly yelled.

Kenneth ducked again behind the big Pittsburgh lady as they neared.

Austin knocked over a stool. He could no longer endure the barking dog and turned on the painted woman. His words were poisonous, slurred, and booming.

"Lord God Almighty, I have told you I have no money, I am not a senator, and I do not know Captain John."

The audience was silent. Tina was temporarily paralyzed. She looked up at the gigantic disheveled man who reeked of whiskey and blue cheese.

She placed her hands on her hips, each still holding a white high-heeled shoe, and said with just enough spite to recover from the sudden change in circumstances, "You don't have to yell."

A surge of nausea pulsed from Austin's intestines, upward through the swill in his belly, and into the throat, burning like the acid from a truck battery. His face contorted like a knife had entered his bowels. Austin reached his arm to the wall to steady himself. Without warning, a spoonful of yellow bile rose up against the laws of gravity, traveled at great speed, and spewed from Austin's open mouth, splattering directly in the cleavage of the short whore.

Before she could respond, Austin McAdoo let out a mighty agonizing yell, "Ahh," and then turned to run. He was at the glass door and out into the Las Vegas night in seconds, a change of scenery so dramatic he wondered for a moment if he'd even thrown up at all, but the taste in his mouth left no mystery.

Austin circled the parking lot, unable to remember where he'd parked, searching for a glimpse of Emily. But she was gone, and when he finally found the car, there was nothing to do but sit inside and examine his busted life. That's where Kenneth found him, wedged in the driver's seat of the little red car, his cantaloupe head down upon the steering wheel, the door wide open. Kenneth sat down in the passenger seat.

A few seconds passed. Without looking up, Austin said wearily, "She took the cats."

Kenneth turned to look in the backseat. "Yeah, she did. But she left some ham."

"I don't care about the ham," Austin mumbled.

"Look," Kenneth said, "if it's any consolation, marriage is obsolete. It served a purpose centuries ago, but in our modern culture, it's primitive. You can't expect people to make a commitment like that, much less honor the commitment.

"I think maybe we should have contract marriages. People obligate themselves to a set period of time, maybe two or three years, and when the contract runs out, if either party doesn't want to renew the contract, it just expires. They go their separate ways. No need for a nasty divorce or some fancy lawyer."

The two men sat in silence for an extended period of time. With his head still down, Austin said, "If you really feel that way, I'm sorry for you. The only woman who ever loved me, the most beautiful woman I've ever seen, walked in on me in a Las Vegas hotel room where I was drunk, underneath perhaps the most unattractive prostitute in the state of Nevada, and now Emily's gone forever. She even took the cats."

Austin leaned up from the steering wheel and looked at Kenneth Mint. He continued, "But you know what? I feel more sorry for you than I feel for myself. Because Emily was right. You don't have a heart. You're a tree, and nobody will even notice when you die of old age."

Austin felt dizzy. He put his head down where it had been before. His mind lost track and drifted to the idea of his mother.

Kenneth's hand slid down to feel the wad of money in his pocket. There was more in the bag resting in his lap. Kenneth almost reached for the door handle. He almost moved his hand from where it rested to the handle of the door. If he had completed the maneuver, just the simple move a few inches to the right, Kenneth Mint would have walked away and never seen Austin McAdoo again for the rest of his life. But his hand stayed where it was.

"You're wrong," Kenneth said.

The sound of the voice in the car brought Austin back to the conversation.

Kenneth said, "We're gonna find her, and when we do, I'll explain what happened, and she'll take you back."

"She'll never take me back," Austin said. "I broke the promise."

"Look, you didn't break the promise, I did. She's not marrying me, she's marrying you. I can't figure the whole thing out, you and Emily. I've looked and looked for the angle, but I can't find it, probably because there is no angle. She loves you, utterly, completely, and totally, and if you let her get away without doing something, you'll spend the rest of your life trying to imagine how happy you would have been, or unhappy, or whatever."

They sat quietly again in the stuffy car. Austin could feel the sticky leather steering wheel on his forehead when he moved slightly left or right.

"What do we do now?" Austin asked.

"Find the girl," Kenneth said. "This is the part where we find the girl."

Part Three

CREMORA WATSON

"Do you want me to tell you something really subversive? Love is everything it's cracked up to be. That's why people are so cynical about it. It really is worth fighting for, being brave for, risking everything for. And the trouble is, if you don't risk anything, you risk even more."

—Erica Jong, American Author

CHAPTER 9

"Where would you go, " Kenneth asked, "if you were alone in Las Vegas in the middle of the night, really pissed off, carrying two cats and a suitcase?"

The thought brought no comfort to Austin McAdoo. He had relinquished the driver's seat, recognizing his inability to bring his big round eyes into focus. The neon lights were blurry and loud.

Kenneth answered his own question, "Maybe the bus station. I saw it on the way in."

Austin's hand rested on the top of his medicine-ball head. "Who rides the bus anymore?"

"You'd be surprised," Kenneth said. "Lots of famous people ride the bus to avoid the paparazzi. Albert Einstein died on a bus between St. Louis and Kansas City. Everybody just thought he was asleep until he started to smell. The actual bus seat is in a museum in Washington, D.C."

"Yeah," Austin said to himself.

There was no sign of Emily in the bus station parking lot. The two men went inside. It resembled a human zoo. Midnight riders lay around, slouched in chairs, sprawled on the floor like monkeys lounging in the shade waiting for something. They ate snacks from machines and talked amongst themselves about where they were going or where they'd been.

Kenneth stood in line at the window. Austin stood nearby with his hand cupped over the crown of his head like a yarmulke. He proceeded to pull his scalp back, causing the black bushy eyebrows to ride up on his forehead.

The man behind the window said, "Next."

He was short, extremely short, perched up on a stool with his oval-shaped head balanced on thin shoulders. The man's mustache appeared unreal, overly thick.

Kenneth said, "We're lookin' for a girl, early twenties, with two cats."

"We don't let cats on the bus, buddy. Do you want a ticket or not?"

"I don't want a ticket. I just want to know if you've seen a girl like that. Yes or no?"

The man-troll furrowed up his brow, feeling quite safe behind the bulletproof glass, and said, "Buddy, do you have any idea the humanity I see every day from this booth? The buffet of genetic freaks, traveling idiots, one-eyed victims of circumstance?"

He leaned up as far as his little body would stretch,

his hot onion breath against the glass, and said in a slow, mocking, monotone voice, "Do you want a ticket or not?"

Kenneth Mint relished confrontation. His options were always greater than the average responsible adult citizen. So without speaking, he stuck the tip of his long index finger deep inside his snout, fished out a booger, and wiped it lovingly on the glass directly in front of the little man's eyes.

There was a moment of silence.

Kenneth said, "Now, unless you come out of that booth and clean it off, you'll spend the rest of your shift looking at my green friend."

There was another brief silence.

From the corner of his eye, Austin recognized a face. A girl's face, familiar, but not immediately placeable. She walked past, wearing a backpack, sandals, and a lime- green bandana on her head.

Inside the booth, the little man picked up the phone to call the police. He would not be outdone. Not on his turf. Not tonight. He would enjoy the last laugh, watching the disgusting pervert led away in handcuffs. He looked away from Kenneth's eyes. Any man who would do such a thing is capable of complete anarchy, he thought, totally beyond reason, so look away until the situation is back under control.

At the sight of the little man reaching for the phone, Austin felt a jolt of adrenaline. He was in no condition to deal with the authorities.

"Let's go," Austin said.

"Why?"

"Because the man is calling the police."

"So what?" Kenneth said calmly. "Boogers are not illegal. They never have been, and they never will be. And you know why?"

Austin grabbed Kenneth by the forearm. "We're not going to worry about why right now. Emily's not here, and we need to leave."

Kenneth held his ground, staring at the little man through the glass.

"Please," Austin begged.

Kenneth allowed himself to be pulled toward the door. Austin broke into a full sprint, his ears cocked for the sound of distant sirens. He reached the car, started the engine, and waited for Kenneth Mint to casually make his way to the vehicle. As he opened the passenger-side door, the shriek of a siren sent Austin's heart into a spasm.

"Get in. Get in," Austin bellowed.

Just as Kenneth's backside hit the seat of the car, Austin gunned the gas and the tires squealed across the parking lot. They were on the road ahead of the siren.

"You've got a serious problem with authority figures, Austin."

Austin's head pounded, "Excuse me if I choose not to accept mental health analysis from a man who just wiped a booger on a ticket booth."

Kenneth hid his smile. "I've got an idea," he said. "I don't think Emily is leaving Las Vegas tonight. She's got too much baggage, and it's too late at night. I think she got herself a room, and she's holed up in that room, and we're not gonna find her tonight."

Kenneth continued, "I think we should go back to our hotel, get a good night's sleep, take a hot shower, enjoy the many amenities, and wake up fresh in the morning."

Austin was exhausted, hung over, and weak. He didn't have the strength to imagine other possibilities, so back to the room they went.

"It smells like Tina in here," Kenneth said.

"Who's Tina?"

"Your hooker."

Austin glanced at Kenneth Mint.

"I'll flip you for the bed," Kenneth said.

Austin gathered his toiletries and began the hygiene ritual.

"Why would you want the bed? It's nighttime, Kenneth. Remember, you're a bat. You stay awake all night."

"Not tonight," Kenneth said. "Tonight, I sleep like a baby in luxury."

Austin hardly recognized himself in the bathroom mirror. His face was swollen and red. He just looked at the puffy skin.

"What have I done?" he said to himself. And then he said it again. "What have I done?"

It seemed like a dream. A weird, disjointed, half-awake dream. The drinks, the prostitute, Emily running out the door, the bus station. Maybe Kenneth was right. Maybe everything would be clearer in the morning.

Austin stepped out of the bathroom to find Kenneth, fully clothed, occupying one-half of the king-size bed.

"You sure do spend a long time in the bathroom, Mr. McAdoo. You must have a lot to work on."

Austin stood in his boxer shorts and yellow bumblebee T-shirt. He said, "I've never been burdened by the belief I'm handsome."

Kenneth thought about the idea.

Austin was too tired to fight over the bed. He crawled under the sheets on his side.

They were quiet for a time. The lights from the lamp on Kenneth's side illuminated the room. Both men felt the oddness of lying in a bed with another man. They were very still.

Austin said, "What if we don't find her?"

Kenneth lay on his back, hands folded across his stomach, staring up at the white ceiling. He said, "Then you'll end up like me."

It was a peculiar statement, a rare opening, and Austin let it linger in the cool air of the room.

"What happened to you?" Austin asked gently.

Kenneth barely heard the question. He had fallen into a crack in his memory, a slip in time, and he began to speak. "I did everything I thought I was supposed to do. I found a girl and married her. I worked hard, paid my bills, got up early in the morning. I didn't smoke dope, or cheat on my wife, or hang out down at the bar. I even remembered her birthday and our anniversary, every time, every single time."

Austin noticed how Kenneth's voice had changed. Distant, as if he were talking to no one in particular, yet strong, like he'd practiced the words inside his head a million times, sounding different in the open air.

"What happened?" Austin asked.

"We had a little girl. Amanda. She was three. She was the best thing. Every morning before I went to work, she wrapped her arms around me like we were falling through the sky together. And when I got home every night, she was standing on the front porch waiting.

"Until Amanda, I had no idea. I hope you find out what I mean."

The two men were silent. Each looked up. There was a loud laugh down the hall. A drunk woman's laugh, sharp like a cackle.

"Where is Amanda?" Austin asked.

Moments passed, until Austin thought there would be no answer.

Kenneth said slowly, "She wanted to go to McDonald's. It was only a few miles away. She loved the Happy Meal. That's what she wanted.

"So I told her I'd take her.

"We were almost there. One block away. When a guy ran through the red light. It happened in a blink of an eye. Just a blink."

The room was quiet again. The drunk lady's laugh was gone. Austin wanted the story to stop. He didn't want to hear any more.

"The guy was just in a hurry. I remember his name. Keith Wingate. He was in a hurry. He ran a red light. And my baby was dead. Just like that."

Austin felt a tightness in his throat. He could feel the wetness pool in his eyes. We just don't know people. We just don't know how they end up where they do, the sadness that forges all of us, hardens some places and leaves others tender and raw.

Austin said, "It wasn't your fault."

Kenneth touched his tongue to his lips, closed his eyes, and said, "What difference does it make? Fault is man-made. Do you think a deer cares whose fault anything is? It doesn't matter. We buried our baby, and the combination of our bodies couldn't survive. She just walked out the door, and left me sittin' on the couch.

"If I had any balls at all, I would have blown my brains out right then, sittin' on the couch. But for some reason, I couldn't do it. So I just wander around. I don't even know what for. Why would anybody want to live in a world where three-year-old little girls die on the way to McDonald's?"

Neither man fell asleep for quite some time, but when they did, each slept soundly. Austin woke up first and called his mother from the bathroom.

"Mom, I asked Emily to marry me."

"What?"

"I asked her to marry me."

"That's what I thought you said. Are you still on

the peyote?"

"Mother, I'm serious. I asked Emily to marry me, and she said 'yes,' but now there's a problem."

"What could be the problem?"

"It's complicated."

"I'm quite sure it's complicated, honey. Life is complicated. Where are you?"

"Las Vegas."

"Where is Emily?"

"She left."

"Left Las Vegas, or left you?"

"Maybe both."

"Give me the short version?"

Austin cringed. "Kenneth planned a bachelor party. I drank too much."

"I've been a woman a long time. We don't usually leave our men for getting drunk at a bachelor party."

Austin shifted his bottom on the flat hard seat of the commode. He cringed again, "Well, there was this lady."

"Lady?" Austin's mother repeated.

"Not really a lady. A prostitute. A middle-aged prostitute. She mistakenly believed I was a senator. It was a big mix-up."

Austin's mother sat in her linoleum kitchen, at her old kitchen table, and smiled at the idea of her introverted son in Las Vegas wrapped in a ball of middle-aged prostitutes, marriage proposals, brown whiskey, and runaway love.

"You know, Austin, you spent most of your years

closed up in this house watching life pass you by out the windows. It looks like you're makin' up for lost time. If you want, me and this nasty poodle will jump in the car and drive out to Las Vegas, Nevada, to help you out of this mess."

Austin took a deep breath. "I don't even know why I called you."

"We've already been through that before. You call me because I'm your mother. The sound of my voice is soothing and comforting."

"No mother, your voice is rough and hoarse."

Lila McAdoo scratched her ass in the privacy of her own home.

"Austin, next time you call me, tell me how you found the girl, and got married, and you can't believe how wonderful this world can be, and you plan to move back to Alabama and give me a shitload of grandkids, with names like Luke and Missy. Can you do that? Now get up off the toilet and go look for her."

"How did you know I was in the bathroom?" he asked.

"How did you know I was in the kitchen?" she responded.

Kenneth Mint's voice boomed, "Get out of the bathroom, pretty boy. My bladder's about to explode."

"Who was that?" Lila asked.

"Nobody. I've got to go."

"By the way," Lila said, "there's a big hurricane coming straight up the Gulf from Cuba. It's off the coast of Tampa, but they say it's coming this way.

Guess what they named the damn thing?"

"I have to go, Mother."

"Austin."

"What?"

"They named it Austin. And it's a Category Four. A beautiful storm. Perfect eye wall. A hundred-and-fifty-mile-an-hour winds. You should see it, like a white spinwheel. Takes up the whole Gulf of Mexico.

Kenneth yelled, "I'm gonna piss in your suitcase."

Lila McAdoo added, "I think it's a sign from God."

Austin hung up the phone as he opened the bathroom door. Kenneth squeezed through the doorframe at the same time as Austin. The two men became momentarily stuck face-to-face like lovers on a moonlit beach. Austin sucked in his belly, releasing the thin man from the intimate wedge.

Kenneth turned on Austin. "Are you tryin' to kill me? Because if you're tryin' to kill me, just say so."

They packed their bags in silence. The absence of Emily and the cats had created a void of sorts, a new dynamic, and after the personal revelations of the night before, and the moment together in the door frame, the men were each slightly lost.

From the passenger seat of the red car, Kenneth turned the knob on the radio. Nothing. He turned again, listening for the click. Again, nothing.

Kenneth inhaled a long exasperated breath. "I don't think I will survive the day without music."

Austin looked over. "I believe you are perhaps the most contradictory person I have ever met. You have no worldly possessions, poor hygiene, and act like you need none of the simple luxuries, and yet, you cannot survive the day without the inane background noise of a local radio station."

Kenneth shot back, "Well you know what, brother Austin, inconsistency is the only common thread amongst cultures, sexes, ages, religions, and head sizes. We strive toward congruity in our beliefs and ideas, but eventually, ultimately, through necessity or laziness, we constantly contradict ourselves. Now let's go have some breakfast before I gag on my own profound understanding of the human condition."

It was as though Emily, and to a lesser extent, Glenn, had served as valuable buffers between the two demanding personalities, and now, left alone, the men rubbed each other like sandpaper.

They sat across from one another in the booth at the Waffle Hut. As usual, Kenneth's back was against the far wall, giving him a clear view of the door. The waitress approached and stood above, white pad and blue pen in her hand. She looked down at the hungry men, stuck out her bottom lip, and then said, "Well good morning, Senator. Captain John."

"Oh my God," Austin said.

Kenneth's eyes grew wide. "Oh my God is right. You work at Waffle Hut?"

Tina made the meanest face she could make. In the light of day Austin could see the thick layer of brownish base make-up and the gray roots in the blonde hair. The memory of her lumpy bare ass appeared like a snapshot and then faded away.

Kenneth released a laugh and sat up straight like a kid in trouble at school.

"He's not really a senator, Tina."

"I ain't stupid," she snorted. "I figured that out."

"He's a Supreme Court Justice," Kenneth said. He smiled a little smile at the toadlike woman and lowered his voice to say, "You know, you're a lot better lookin' in the daytime."

She said, "And you owe me money, whatever your name is."

"Pay the woman, Austin," Kenneth said earnestly.

"I'll do no such thing."

"I'm callin' the damn cops," she said and turned her body to the phone.

Austin was immediately struck by the familiar wave of fear, his body instantly sucked dry of energy, his head floating in a bath of warm fluid. He heard his voice say, "No."

So Tina Louise Dalrimple stopped. She went back to the table and held out her red-palmed hand. Austin put money in the leathery palm. His predicament sickened him, but the alternative was hardly an alternative at all. The prospect of being questioned by the local authorities in Waffle Hut concerning the events of the night before, in the company of the toad-waitress and Kenneth Mint, sent shivers up his sternum.

Austin rubbed the moisture from his forehead. "Please bring me a large number of waffles with extra syrup, a whole tomato, and chocolate milk."

Tina looked at Kenneth Mint. He said, "I'll have one raw egg and a glass of warm apple juice."

She walked away with a smirk.

Kenneth said to Austin, "She's gonna spit in your chocolate milk."

Austin said to no one in particular, "Please God, get me through this day, and I will do as you ask."

The men sat waiting for their food.

Kenneth said, "Have I ever told you about my friend, Ray?"

Austin's face remained expressionless.

"Well, anyway, my friend Ray decided he was gonna kill himself. He just didn't want to live anymore. And for some crazy reason, he decided he wanted to do it on the railroad tracks.

"So he found out what time the next train was comin' through town, and he went down to the railroad tracks behind the hardware store to wait. He figured if he laid his head on the tracks, it would be painless, and for some reason, he thought it would be better if it looked like an accident."

Austin listened with a blank face. A young woman passed the table on the way to the bathroom. He recognized the lime-green bandana he had seen on the familiar girl at the bus station the night before.

"So Ray saw the train comin' a mile away. He got down on his knees, bent over, and laid his neck on the hot steel track. He thought about all the reasons he wanted to die, and the way they'd find his body mutilated in the rocks, and waited.

"The train got closer and closer, and he could feel the power of the engine in the metal beneath his head. But the train was slowing down, and Ray prayed it wouldn't stop. The big wheels kept turning, and Ray kept praying, until the giant train was only a hundred yards away, and then fifty, and then twenty-five.

"Ray pushed his neck down on the track and awaited his fate. He watched the train decelerate, ever so slowly, ten feet away, five feet, and he anticipated the end. But the first steel wheel of the engine inched up to Ray and came to a complete stop just as it pinched the flesh of Ray's neck between the big steel wheel and the smooth iron traintrack."

Austin hated himself for caring how the story would end.

"And so there he was, down on his knees. A sharp pain shooting from the skin pinched between the wheel and the track. He tried to pull away, stretching the skin, but it wouldn't let loose. He started screaming, 'Back it up. Back up the train. For the love of God.'"

Austin wished his waffles would arrive.

"But you just can't back up a train like that. It takes time," Kenneth added.

The bathroom door opened. The young woman with the lime-green bandana headed toward Austin McAdoo. He knew her. He knew he knew her. And she looked at him. And she recognized the oversized head and jet-black wavy hair.

The woman stopped at the table.

Austin said, "Cremora?"

Cremora asked, "Fat guy from my apartment?"

And Kenneth Mint felt a tingle. A flutter in his chest.

CHAPTER 10

"What are you doing here?" Austin asked Cremora.

"Let me guess," Cremora said, "Emily's gone."

"How did you know that?"

"What did you expect from a girl who quit her job, packed her bags, and ran off in the middle of the night with somebody like you? Did you consider that to be the act of a stable, rational human being?"

Austin hadn't thought about Emily in such a way. For Austin, spontaneous and irrational had conveniently drifted apart from one another since the moment Emily had sat down in his car. It just made sense.

"What are you doing here?" Austin repeated, his reactions dulled by the funk of a smelly hangover.

"You're mother told me where you were going. Besides, there's a hurricane in the Gulf. A big son-of-a-bitch, named Austin as a matter of fact. Let's not pretend it's a coincidence. People started evacuating. I evacuated to Las Vegas. You might as well go someplace more interesting than Valdosta, Georgia. Besides, the Weather Channel is everywhere now. You can watch your home get destroyed from the safety and security of a hotel room two thousand miles away. It's not officially reality TV unless it's your stuff actually being swept into the raging waters of the Gulf of Mexico."

Kenneth Mint couldn't stop staring at her mouth as she spoke. It was small and quick. The lips moved with purpose and precision.

"What are you staring at?"

"Your mouth. It's fantastic."

Cremora, still standing, bent her attention to Kenneth. She said, "My mother explained to me a long time ago, if a male and a female bear run into each other in the woods, the survival of the species demands they copulate. If both were equally driven to hump, they would inevitably fight about who's on top, et cetera. The bickering would spoil the mood and the bears would simply drift apart, going their own ways without doing their share to insure the existence of bears.

"So one bear, the male, was selected to be blinded and stupified by the desire to screw. He's bigger and stronger, so he can have his way with minimal bickering or resistance. The female bear was chosen to have a vivid imagination so she can think about other things while she's being violated. She's also programmed to remain rational during the act, carry the baby in her womb, use her superior intellect to select a safe home, and provide for her cub. In the meantime, Horny Harry is wandering around the woods porkin' whatever moves."

Kenny was mesmerized. Cremora concluded, "You, my friend, will never see or touch my privates, no matter how rich, or dashing, or humorous, you turn out to be. So tuck your bear penis back in your pouch."

Austin said, "Will you help us find Emily? We're getting married."

She looked at Kenneth. "Scoot over." And he did, making room in the booth on his side.

Tina arrived with food. She set down the plates and looked at Cremora. "Don't let 'em screw ya, honey. This one ain't no senator, and this one ain't no captain. I didn't figure it out until I was buck naked ridin' Moby Dick here."

In the most condescending tone imaginable, Cremora Watson said to Austin, "Did you say something about getting married?"

Austin looked down at his waffle, hoping for Tina to go away. She waited, arms crossed, believing she had found an ally in the odd-looking woman with the lime-green bandana.

Austin looked up at the waitress, and they locked eyes for a long, exasperating period of discomfort. He could taste whiskey on the fat part of his tongue.

Austin could wait no longer. "Go, please. Go

anywhere."

She stood her ground, tapping the toe of her little white tennis shoe against the beige tile floor.

"You don't fool me," she finally said.

Austin felt himself ready to explode, but he was aware of the pitfalls of the situation, the potential to alienate Cremora, whom he needed, by attacking a woman he'd seen naked in a hotel room the day after he proposed marriage to Emily, a woman who simply refused to go away.

"Please," Austin begged.

Tina stuck out her bottom lip like her point had been made. She turned and walked away, a little extra swing in her hips.

Austin set about explaining himself. "It's complicated."

Kenneth looked at Cremora's hands folded together on the top of the table. They were soft and small, the nails chewed to the quick.

"It was a bachelor party," Austin said. "Things went wrong. Kenneth went too far."

Cremora turned to look at the man beside her. Kenneth Mint shrugged his shoulders and made a face of misunderstanding.

"Your hands are quite nice," he said.

Cremora rolled her eyes and waited for the remainder of Austin's excuse.

"It's complicated. I guess all I can say is, 'I'm sorry.' I want to marry Emily. We got engaged at the Grand Canyon. She's the only thing I've ever really wanted.

Everything before her seems remote and stupid."

There was silence between the three.

"Tell me the bear story again," Kenneth said.

Cremora was focused on Austin. Austin looked down at the cold waffles.

"I love her," he said to himself, and then couldn't believe the words had come from his mouth.

The man across from Cremora was simply huge. Her eyes scanned him for signals of insincerity. There were none.

"I believe you," Cremora said.

"You do?"

"Yeah, I do. I don't have to understand it to believe it's true."

Kenneth had forgotten about his delicious breakfast of warm apple juice and a raw egg in a white bowl.

"What do you really know about Emily?" she asked Austin.

She answered her own question. "Nothing, I bet."

Cremora said, "When she was six years old, one morning, her mother and father just got in the car and drove away. They weren't killed in some horrible accident, or murdered by devil worshippers. They just told Emily to play with her doll for a minute while they went to the store for cigarettes. And they never came back. Ever."

Even Kenneth followed the story.

Cremora continued, "Some people are devoid of the stuff that makes us worthwhile. She never saw her parents again. They never came back. They never called. They never even sent a card.

"And so Emily came to live with us when she was about seven. Our mothers are sisters. She grew up in my home, but there was always something missing. When she got older, starting in high school, she'd wander off in different directions, like she was looking for something but didn't have a single clue what it was, or where it could be.

"She'd always come back home. This is the longest she's been gone."

Austin listened. When the story ended, he spoke from his heart for the first time since he was a small child, unafraid for reasons he couldn't possibly explain. "I wish I could say I'm what she's been looking for. Maybe she's just been looking for somebody who's been looking for her. And I can say without a doubt, that's me.

"Will you help us find her?" Austin asked as a sudden pang of nausea invaded his belly.

Cremora stared into the big man's face. She seemed to be reading something written just below the first layer of his skin. Finally she said, "You don't seem like the same jackass who stood in my kitchen last week."

Kenneth said, "He's a different jackass."

Both Austin and Cremora turned to Kenneth Mint. The Waffle Hut was alive with strange intentions and wounded creatures.

Finally Cremora said, "We all get left sooner or later, Austin. It's what we do afterwards that counts. Let's go find Emily."

Kenneth held the white bowl to his lips and drank the single raw egg. As they stood to leave, Austin found himself incapable of abandoning one particular round waffle. He held it in his hand at his side like it was perfectly normal to carry a waffle in such a way.

Tina stood across the cash register from Austin. For a moment, it was as though no one else was around. Only a few short hours earlier they had been slightly intimate in a Las Vegas hotel room. Now they were like strangers, which, in fact, is exactly what they were.

Tina took the twenty dollar bill from Austin. She didn't notice the waffle in his other hand. She gave Austin his change, and as he counted the last two dimes, Tina said, "I had a good time last night."

Austin looked up at the woman in her Waffle Hut uniform. Immersed in his private hangover, he truly could summon no response, and as he walked away, no response came to him. He merely thought, "What could she mean by such a statement?"

Kenneth took his customary position in the backseat of the little red car. Cremora sat in the passenger seat and watched curiously as Austin contorted through the ritual of entering the cockpit.

"Can you run by the bus station so I can get my stuff out of the locker?" she asked.

From the backseat, Kenneth declared, "I spent a year in Oregon looking for Bigfoot."

When there was no response, Kenneth said, "We slept in tents during the day and at night we got out all the equipment - night vision goggles, motion sensors. There's a whole group of people who stay up there in a camp in the woods, go home to their families, and back to the camp. Two weeks on, two weeks off, like working on an oil rig."

Austin noticed the difference in the tone of Kenneth's voice. It was a bit more high-pitched, boasting.

Cremora turned to look at Kenneth.

He said, sitting up straighter than usual, "One time I thought I saw him. At night, that's when they forage. I was stationed in a tree. I heard a sound, like a twig snapping. I waited. It got closer.

"I think I saw him. He was about Austin's size. Everybody thinks Bigfoot's hairy, but he's not. He's white-skinned, pale, smooth, and hairless. That's why he hides in the daytime. Too easy to see. He only goes out at night."

Cremora took a slow, deep breath.

Kenneth concluded, "Anyway, I wasn't scared of him."

Cremora let the last sentence hang for a while. She turned around and tried to click on the radio.

"It doesn't work," Austin said.

Cremora turned the knob to increase the airflow from the air conditioner. The fan blew a loud gust of frigid air, sputtered, and then abruptly stopped.

"Oh, shit," Kenneth muttered.

Cremora said, "Air-conditioning makes you weak anyway. It destroys your natural immune system. The sudden change in temperature just isn't something our bodies usually experience in nature. Roll down the windows."

Austin pushed the buttons on the door to roll down the electric windows down. Nothing moved. He tried again. Nothing moved.

"Oh, shit," Kenneth said again.

Austin slammed the armrest on the door with his clenched fist. His state of mind was weak, and the blood pounded rhythmically in his sealed head like a pump. As the heat reached a stifling level inside the car, Austin parked outside the bus station.

"I'll be back in a minute," Cremora said, and left the two men in the sauna.

"What do you think of her?" Kenneth asked.

"Who?"

"The girl, Cremora. Who the hell do you think?"

"I believe she better hurry, or I may die of heat stroke."

There was a pause. Kenneth asked, "Was that Bigfoot story stupid? It sounded kinda stupid, didn't it? Tell the truth."

Austin was dizzy. He opened his door a crack, but the air outside provided no relief. Cremora arrived carrying her backpack. In her hand she held two well-worn paperback books.

"All right, first let's try the souvenir shops. Emily loves a souvenir. We'll work our way toward the airport," she ordered.

Kenneth inched up in his seat to get a look at the

books in Cremora's lap. He squinted over her shoulder to read the titles. In red letters against a black background he could read, *Monkey Graveyard*. He bent his head to the left to see the spine of the second book, *Shetland Pony Girl*.

"What's with the books?" Kenneth asked.

"They're for reading. That's what books are for. You're probably a movie guy. I bet you haven't read a book since you were forced in high school, and then you probably read the Cliffs Notes.

"It's the major dividing line between people. Those who read books, and those who don't. Movies are for people too lazy to utilize their own imaginations. So they sit back and watch someone else's imagination on the screen. Listen to someone else's thoughts. Do you know we burn less calories watching television than we do while we sleep? You know why? Because at least while we're asleep our minds are forced to imagine through dreams. When we watch a movie, or television, we're like zombies. No wonder America is the fattest country in the history of the world."

Sweat poured down Austin's forehead in little rivers, around his eyes, over the hills and valleys of his nose and cheeks, and dripped hotly off the edges of his face onto his nylon shorts. Each drip made a small noise.

"Can I see *Monkey Graveyard*?" Kenneth asked.

Cremora handed him the book over her shoulder without turning around.

She said, mostly to Austin, "Do you know what

the single most interesting tangible thing on this planet is?"

Without a conscious thought, Austin blurted out, "Silly putty?"

Cremora didn't hear him and said over the top of his words, "A person. A person, a single human is the most interesting tangible thing on this planet."

From the backseat Kenneth said, "I thought they just buried monkeys in the woods."

Austin pulled into the parking lot in front of the first cheesy souvenir shop he saw. Cremora jumped out.

Kenneth said, "Listen to this crazy shit," and he began reading to Austin from the paperback book. "If I were a stingray, I would use my whiplike tail to remove the feet of the giant monkeys who venture into the waters for a meal of shellfish. I would eat the bloody feet, digest the flesh, and crap out a new monkey. Maybe one with no feet at all."

The two men contemplated the paragraph. Kenneth said, "She underlined that part. Why?"

Austin wiped his brow. Cremora entered the steamy car.

"We got lucky. She was here earlier this morning. She bought a pair of red and gold dice. The man remembered the cats. He said she talked about Los Angeles."

Austin perked up slightly. "Los Angeles? That's where we were planning to be married. On Hollywood Boulevard, the Julia Roberts star."

"I believe it," Cremora said. "Let's go straight to the airport. She wasn't at the bus station. Maybe she's gonna fly."

Austin peeled out of the parking lot like he'd seen people do on television. Out on the road, Kenneth said, "I see here you've underlined a passage in your book. I was wondering why."

"Is it the part about the stingray?" she asked.

"Yes."

"It's an analogy. It's all just a matter of what people are willing to do. Some people are willing to murder or rape. Others aren't willing to get up off the couch to go to the grocery store. What are you willing to do? That's the question you have to ask yourself."

Kenneth said, "I'm willing to shave every hair from my body if you ask me to."

There was another pause in the stagnant car.

Cremora spun around to face Kenneth. "Who exactly are you again?"

"I'm Kenneth. Kenneth Mint. It's not like my hair is doing me much good anyway. If you ask, I'll shave all of it off."

Cremora looked up to see the police station over to the right.

"Pull in here," she said.

Austin did as he was told, operating primarily on fumes of hope as his body slowly dehydrated.

"Why?" he mumbled.

"I'm gonna make sure she hasn't been arrested or picked up for some reason."

Austin parked between two police cruisers. In his weakened condition, he slowly began to feel the onset of anxiety associated with proximity to law enforcement. His heart picked up speed and he actually began to pant like a St. Bernard.

Kenneth said, "Do you have a razor?"

A stout police officer exited the front door and walked in Austin's direction. He immediately made eye contact with Austin and held the gaze. Austin looked away as the officer circled the car, stopped at the rear and jotted down the license plate number. The officer went back inside the station.

Austin wiped his brow again, clearing the little rivers of sweat, making way for new little rivers to form. He caught himself panting and closed his mouth.

"Do you have a razor?" Kenneth repeated.

"Shut up," Austin whispered under his breath.

"Don't tell me to shut up."

Austin tried to turn his head to look at Kenneth. Before he could say another word, there was a sharp tap on the glass of the driver's side window.

"Roll down your window," the officer said.

Austin fumbled for the button on the armrest and then remembered the windows didn't work. He held up his hands and smiled poorly.

The officer opened Austin's door.

"Can I help you gentlemen?" the officer asked.

Kenneth said, "Yeah, I'll have a cheeseburger and some crispy golden fries."

"He's just kidding," Austin said.

"May I see your driver's license, sir?"

Kenneth was reading *Monkey Graveyard*. With his eyes still on the book he said, "Don't give him shit, Austin. Tell him you know your constitutional rights."

Austin started to negotiate the angles to remove his wallet from his back pocket and then remembered his license was lost, left on the floorboard of the Alabama state trooper's car days ago. He began to wet himself a little.

"I lost it."

"Excuse me?"

"I lost my license."

"Sir, could you come inside the station with me for a minute?"

Austin's head floated from his body. His limbs were heavy like the trunks of trees. He felt himself move, and then stand, and then Austin saw himself from above as he followed the officer into the station.

"Have a seat, please."

Austin collapsed into a chair. He heard his voice say, "My name is Austin McAdoo."

Cremora appeared in the lobby.

"Why didn't you wait in the car?" she said to Austin. "Emily's not here."

Austin didn't answer.

The officer came through a door and stood above Austin.

"Mr. McAdoo, we've got a hit on your name and vehicle. Apparently, it involves the death of a police officer in Alabama a few days ago."

Cremora said, "Please tell me you're not a murderer. Please tell me that you and your weird friend didn't kill Emily and bury her in the desert."

The officer asked, "Who's Emily?"

Austin released a low grunting noise before he fell sideways and slammed against the floor of the police station lobby. The chair shot from his backside and tumbled over.

Cremora made no movement whatsoever. The officer got down on bended knee to assist the gigantic man on the floor who was panting again.

Cremora said, with arms crossed, "Is he a murderer?"

The policeman helped Austin to an upright sitting position, with his back against the wall. When it appeared Austin had simply passed out and would recover, the police officer answered Cremora's question. "I think he fainted. No, ma'am, he's not a murderer, at least not to my knowledge. The state trooper in Alabama apparently died of natural causes. They found Mr. McAdoo's driver's license in the trooper's car. A bulletin was issued asking law enforcement to be on the lookout for Mr. McAdoo or his car. They just told me on the phone the trooper's widow wanted to talk to Mr. McAdoo. Wanted to ask him something."

Cremora listened intently. She bent down and used both of her hands to pinch Austin's fleshy cheeks. "Wake up. A lady wants to talk to you. We've got things to do."

Cremora said to the officer, "Could you get the lady on the phone and bring the phone to Austin? I don't think he's gonna move anytime soon."

The officer left, and Austin began to regain his faculties. It was as if he were crawling through a dark pipe toward a light at the end.

"Where am I?" he mumbled.

"In a police station, in Las Vegas, passed out on the floor, getting ready to talk on the phone to the widow of the dead state trooper."

Austin had the taste of canned ham in his mouth. The officer handed Austin the telephone.

"Hello," he said.

"Mr. McAdoo?"

"Yes."

"This is Trudy Nixon," the voice said softly.

"Trudy Nixon," Austin repeated.

"Yes. My husband, Tom, recently died of a heart attack. He was an Alabama trooper. He loved his job. Your mother told us you were dead."

The woman's voice trailed away. Austin looked at his shoes.

She continued after a moment. "It's been very hard on us. Tom was a good father. He was young. It's just hard to understand why God would take him away from us for no reason."

There was a moment of silence. "Are you there?" she asked.

"Yes," Austin managed to say.

The woman continued, "Anyway, I know it's crazy, but they tell me you're probably the last person to talk to Tom. I was just wondering what you talked about. What he might have said."

Austin rubbed his eyes with his free hand. Sitting in the air conditioned lobby, he could actually feel his thoughts coming back together.

"Well," Austin said, "he talked about you, and the kids, and said something about football, I think."

The woman made a noise on the other end of the line, but Austin couldn't tell if she was crying.

"He told me how much he loved you, and the children, and then he told me to slow down, and not drive so fast, because I might end up mutilated on the side of the highway and never get a chance to have a wife and family like his."

Austin imagined the woman smiling with tears in her eyes. He could picture her clearly in his mind, petite, good complexion, wearing a yellow sundress.

Then she asked, "Did he say anything about the whore he'd been screwin' in the trailer park?"

Austin looked up at Cremora and the police officer above. The visual image of the widow vanished. He was very thirsty.

" No, I don't remember anything about a girl in the trailer park."

"Good." she said. "That's good."

There was a long stretch of quiet.

"Can I go now?" Austin asked.

"Yes, thank you," the soft voice said, and the

conversation was over. The woman was left alone to think her own thoughts.

Cremora helped Austin to his feet and they made it back to the car. Kenneth was entrenched in Chapter two of *Monkey Graveyard*. He'd lost track of time and place, carried by the words of the book, undoubtedly burning huge numbers of calories in the process.

When they finally arrived at the airport, Cremora announced, "Okay, it's a pain in the ass getting information about passengers from the airlines, so here's the story. Emily's my sister, our father just died, and I need to find her immediately."

Kenneth said, "How'd your father die?"

"He didn't really die, idiot. It's just a story."

"I realize it's just a story, but you need to have details. It sounds less like a lie when you have details."

Cremora conceded. "Okay, then he died of poison."

"Poison?" Kenneth asked.

"Yeah, poison."

"What kind of poison?" Kenneth asked.

"Never mind," Cremora screamed. "You two sit in the car. I'll be back."

The men opened both doors to let any breeze enter. Kenneth sank into his book like a man in a pool of quicksand, slowly and entirely. Austin fell asleep and dreamed he was in a field of rabbits.

Cremora slammed the car door, waking Austin from his rabbits and instantly sucking Kenneth up from the quicksand.

"She flew to Los Angeles. We missed her by thirty

minutes. Let's hit the road, fat boy."

A few miles down Interstate 15 Kenneth said from the backseat, "Did they ask you what kind of poison?"

Cremora didn't answer. She didn't feel like it. Instead, she opened *Shetland Pony Girl* and started where she left off.

CHAPTER 11

The shrill sound of the butt whistle split the silence inside the car. Austin's face froze like a high school kid in class, embarrassed for the perpetrator, and at the same time afraid of the prospect of false accusation. Cremora looked up from the page of her book and then back down. The whistle blew again, a little louder and longer, pulling Cremora's head around to the back seat.

"What's that noise?"

Kenneth casually looked up from a particularly unusual section of *Monkey Graveyard*.

"What noise?"

The sun reflected on the cracked rear window catching Cremora's attention.

"What happened to the window?"

Kenneth turned around as if he'd never seen it before and said, "The people guarding the world's largest chicken busted it with a rock."

"Why?" she asked.

Kenneth said, "Because Austin murdered the world's largest chicken. I saw it, and I'll never forget it."

Austin was still emerging from his hangover. "Lord, no, it was an accident."

Kenneth had an idea. He swivelled his long body into an upside down position, feet to the roof, cocked his knees, and kicked both heels into the cracked window, sending a large chunk of shattered glass flying into the air and exploding like ice on the highway.

Austin shrieked like an elderly woman. Kenneth swivelled back upright and announced, "It was hot." He immediately located his place on the page where he left off, spotting the word "titillation."

Austin yelled, "This is *my* car, not yours. *You* don't have a car. *You* don't have anything. I don't even know why you're here."

Kenneth responded, enunciating his words very clearly, "Let me ask you this question, Austin. When you pull off a lizard's tail, it grows back. The tail actually grows back on the end of the lizard. How come the leftover tail doesn't grow a new lizard? Can you explain that? Why doesn't it go both ways?"

Austin's blood pressure brought the pounding back to the top of his skull, convincing him a stroke was certainly imminent.

Cremora glanced at the gas gauge. "We're almost out of gas."

Austin focused his bloodshot eyes on the dashboard instruments. The needle was on the bad side of the faded "e."

"Oh my God," he muttered, looked up in a panic, and yanked the car to the right and down an exit ramp.

"Who's got gas money?" Cremora asked.

"Not me," Kenneth answered quickly. "I refuse to support the use of fossil fuels."

"Do you have a better idea?" Cremora asked.

"As a matter of fact, I do. The ultimate alternative fuel source. You know what it is? Dead people. We have an endless supply. And if our demand outstretches the natural supply, we can grow humans in warehouses the size of football fields.

"Think about it. We can harvest people with no heads, genetically designed to be headless, without thoughts and therefore without souls. It's no different than genetically altered cows, bred to have more delicious milk or more tender meat.

"Of course, I know what you're thinking. It's a moral dilemma. Do we utilize the headless fuel cells while they're still alive and kicking, or are we ethically bound to euthanize the mutants before they're fed into the engine? But without heads, or brains, there's no pain, right? And you certainly can't hurt their feelings.

"Sooner or later, we also have to face the racial issue. It's a scientific fact that French Canadians provide a cleaner fuel source. Is that fact a slap in the face to all other races, or will the French Canadians protest the harvesting of their people?"

Cremora listened to the soliloquy. "I'm curious Mr. Mint, have you ever self-mutilated or forgotten to wear clothes?"

Kenneth cocked his head. "Ma'am, over these last hours, I've come to the realization that you'll never feel about me the way I feel about you, but I don't think this fact has to be fatal to our future. If one side of a relationship is especially strong, do you think it can survive? Could you be satisfied with a one-sided relationship?"

Austin spotted a gas station up ahead. He passed a green sign that read, "Mojave National Preserve." Kenneth waited patiently for an answer. The silence lasted long enough to make him believe Cremora would completely ignore the question.

Then she said, "Maybe."

Kenneth felt the pressure at the front end of the butt whistle. He tightened until the pressure subsided.

Cremora and Austin paid for a full tank of gas, used the bathrooms, and bought two cold Diet Cokes while Kenneth sat alone in the car thinking about the change in circumstances. On page seventy-seven of *Monkey Graveyard*, he read, "Life is for the present tense. The future is uncertain, beyond control. The past is long gone. Besides, you don't even remember 99% of everything you've done, or seen, or said, and there's very little rhyme or reason to explain the 1% we do carry with us. Don't try to figure it out. Just exist in the only tense available to you, the right now."

The car started. Austin had a flash of hope, tried the windows again, and felt the hope escape slowly like a bad smell. He turned onto the road and drove.

"When we get to Los Angeles, where are we going first?" Austin asked Cremora. He was thinking about Emily, alone, somewhere in the big city. He remembered the look in her eyes, the last look, and the guilt made his face draw up.

"I think she'll go to Hollywood Boulevard. She's talked about it all her life. That's where we should start."

Kenneth saw Cremora's full name written on the inside cover of the paperback book. He said, "Maybe this would be a good time, Ms. Watson, for you to give Austin here a few tips about the honeymoon night. Because if we are successful in locating Emily, and we can get these two kids back together, Mr. McAdoo could be faced with the prospect of marital relations. It's my belief he may be limited in this area."

Austin felt his face redden. He was unsure how to respond, so he stared straight ahead as if the act of driving suddenly demanded his total attention.

Cremora didn't hesitate, "Well, it's a very complicated hole, that's for sure, but don't overestimate the damn thing. It's still just a hole."

Austin had never heard a woman speak so bluntly about those forbidden parts. He continued to stare straight ahead down the long road stretching forever through the middle of the soft brown desert.

"Where the hell are we?" Kenneth asked. "Where's

Interstate 15? That's what we took out of Las Vegas. It's a straight shot to LA."

Austin glanced at Cremora. He tried to remember how he had gotten to the gas station and which way he turned back on the road, and then he looked up to the sun in the sky to try and get his bearings like a lost hunter.

"Where the hell are we?" Kenneth repeated.

Austin defended himself loudly. "I can't do everything. I can't drive and worry about gas and keep up with the map."

"There's no map, " Kenneth said.

Austin bellowed, "Where's the map?"

Kenneth said, "You ate the map, you fat bastard."

The front right tire exploded like a shotgun blast. Some tires leak slowly. Some go flat in silence and cause the car to wobble. This tire blew out like a birthday balloon, pieces shooting in different directions, black streams of rubber spinning into the sand.

Austin grasped the steering wheel, slammed on the brakes, and the wounded car lumbered to a pathetic standstill.

Kenneth said, "That was some crazy shit. Who knows how to change a tire?"

Austin couldn't catch his breath. His body had reached and crossed boundaries of stress and tribulation never before considered possible. Austin sucked in a cubic yard of air wondering if it might be his last oxygen. Kenneth crawled out the back window, squeezing through the hole in the glass like the car was giving birth to a full grown, man-sized bird.

Austin had never changed a tire in his life. He watched his mother do it once, when he was a kid, on the side of the road in Florida, but all he could remember was a feeling of helplessness. He removed himself from the car and walked to the trunk area where he met Cremora.

"Where did all this ham come from?"

Austin said, "I'm a canned ham salesman. Rather, I should say, I used to be a canned ham salesman. I resigned to travel with Emily."

Kenneth wandered into the desert, searching for a fascinating location to urinate. He began to do his business, trying, as usual, to urinate his name in the sand while imagining the feasibility of making a new wheel for the car out of wood. Kenneth looked out across the barren landscape. At a great distance, in the haze of the summer heat, he saw something small moving in his direction. Kenneth squinted his eyes and moved his head in order to see better. He kept his eyes on the movement as he finished and zipped. It was a dog. A small dog. A Benji look-alike. Running at a good clip. Holding something in his mouth. Kenneth stood his ground and watched the small dog get closer and closer. He could hear the sounds of the tire tools behind, but didn't turn to look. A dog in the desert was much more interesting and glorious. He thought, "How far has this dog come? How many days and nights has he traveled through the hot sands to get where he's supposed to be?"

The dog came directly to Kenneth. In his mouth he held a package of small, white powdered doughnuts. The kind every kid loves. The dog dropped the package gently at the feet of Kenneth Mint. Kenneth looked at the doughnuts, at the dog, and then back at the doughnuts.

"I'll make a deal with you," he said. "In exchange for your doughnuts, your only worldly possession, you can ride in our car to Los Angeles. After that, I can't promise anything."

The dog seemed to understand the agreement and nodded his head slightly as a sign of ratification. Kenneth bent down and picked up his doughnuts. He ate the doughnuts, one by one, as the dog watched. After all, Kenneth thought, that was the deal, and the doughnuts were unbelievably delicious. When he was finished, he picked up the dog and went back to the car where Cremora was bent down on one knee tightening the last nut on the undersized spare tire.

Cremora looked up at the two men peering down at her. "It's nice to be with such handy men. If I left you two here on the side of the road, do you think you'd survive through the night?"

"No," Austin said and immediately wished he hadn't. He noticed the dog in Kenneth's arms. "That dog is not entering my vehicle."

"We don't have a choice," Kenneth said.

Austin repeated, "We don't have a choice?"

"No, I'm sorry. We reached an agreement. I'm

bound by a contractual obligation to transport him to Los Angeles in exchange for good and valuable consideration."

Cremora asked, "What was the good and valuable consideration?"

Kenneth looked down at the dog. "I'd rather not say."

Austin raised his voice two octaves. "You expect me to give a stray dog a ride to Los Angeles because you reached an agreement on the side of the road with this animal?"

Kenneth contemplated the question. "Yes."

"You're an idiot. I tell you what, you stay here with your new companion. You've caused nothing but problems since the first minute you entered my life. I've come to the conclusion that *you* are the common denominator underneath each negative event. It's time for us to part ways."

Kenneth looked down at Cremora. She glanced up in his direction as she lowered the car to the ground, turn by turn. When the tire touched the earth, Kenneth went to the back of the red car, slammed the trunk closed, and crawled into the car with the dog in his arms and nestled back in his place amongst the canned hams, hair coat, and empty snack bags.

Austin opened the car door and leaned inside as best he could. "Get out of the car, Kenneth."

"I can't possibly do it, Austin. I'd like to help you, but I can't. God has spoken to me and He said, loud and clear, 'Kenneth, don't get out of the car. You and the dog are needed in Los Angeles. Don't let anything stop you'."

Austin noticed white powder on Kenneth's upper lip. Kenneth saw Austin glance at his lip and sent his tongue exploring the area, rewarded with the sweet taste of powdered sugar. Neither man mentioned the exchange.

"Kenneth, on the first opportunity, I will leave you, regardless of what message you believe God has given. You are a disgusting man."

Kenneth wished he'd left the fat bastard in Las Vegas and taken the money. He watched Cremora and Austin get in the car, and he stared at the back of Austin's head, imagining the flat end of a shovel slamming against the ink-black hair.

As they rode in silence, Kenneth saw a spider crawling up the back of Austin's seat. It was a small spider with what looked to be a tiny horn on its head. It moved up quickly and then stopped on Austin's shoulder. The spider veered left and Kenneth stuck out his index finger, herding the spider back northward in Austin's direction. The spider got off track to the right and again was redirected by Kenneth's thin finger to the target of Austin's neck area.

Kenneth and the panting dog watched closely as the angry little spider reached the collar of Austin's shirt. There was a brief hesitation, and then the horned spider disappeared over the edge of the collar and moved unseen into the double extra-large cotton shirt, making his way to the silver-dollar-sized left nipple of the unaware driver.

Austin felt a tickle and scratched the area, infuriating the spider and causing the little evil beast to bite down with tiny teeth into the nipple flesh of Austin McAdoo.

The big man released a howl of Biblical magnitude, slapped his chest with both hands, and sent the car wildly left, and then right, as Cremora reached for the wheel and the dog buried his face into the pungent armpit of Kenneth.

Austin slammed on the brakes and brought the car to a sudden halt halfway in the soft sand. His heart palpitated, stopped, and started again at a breakneck pace.

"What happened?" Cremora yelled. "What happened?"

"I've been bitten. My nipple."

Kenneth was unable to refrain from smiling as he imagined the spider attached to the tip of Austin's sensitive pink appendage.

"I can't breathe," he gasped.

Cremora was fast to act. "Let me drive. Get out. Let me drive."

She jumped out of the passenger side, ran around the front of the car, and arrived at the driver's door. Austin was pulling his great weight across the console to the passenger's seat and having a difficult time making headway. Cremora pushed with both hands against his mountainous back until Austin was finally out of the way enough for Cremora to drive.

She drove a hundred miles an hour. Austin was incoherently moaning like a sickly moose. Against his wishes, Kenneth began to worry about the moaning man up front. There was a turn, and a sign, and finally a hospital. The red car skidded into a pole outside the door of the emergency room.

Cremora turned to Kenneth. "Get off your lazy ass and help me."

Kenneth did as he was told, leaving the dog and climbing out the back window. He helped Cremora get Austin partially out of the car. Two hospital employees showed up to assist. Austin was limp and sweaty. His ass was too wide for the wheelchair, and Austin rolled over to the ground. Eventually, with additional assistance and determination, Austin's body ended up in a room with a Middle Eastern doctor and a nurse with one blue eye and one brown eye.

"What happened?" the doctor asked Cremora.

"I don't know. He just grabbed his chest. He said he'd been bitten."

Kenneth added, "I think it was a spider."

The doctor asked, "Is he allergic to any medication?"

Cremora and Kenneth looked at each other. Cremora shrugged her shoulders. Austin mumbled, "I'm allergic to relish."

Kenneth said sharply, "Relish isn't a medication, doofus."

The doctor pulled up Austin's shirt. The left nipple was inflamed and there was noticeable swelling of the breast, taking on the appearance of a D-cup.

"Oh my God," Kenneth said.

The doctor asked, "Could you two wait in the lobby? I'll come give you an update when we know something."

On the way down the hall Kenneth asked, "Did you see that?"

"Yes," she said, and then continued, "How did you know it was a spider?"

"Spiders kill more people worldwide than any other single insect or mammal."

"Oh," Cremora said.

Kenneth got the dog out of the car and sat in the clean lobby next to Cremora. The dog enjoyed being rubbed on his head and closed his eyes in ecstasy.

Cremora said, "I'm worried about Austin. What if he dies?"

"I guess you'll have to drive."

Cremora shook her head. "What is the matter with you? Really? What happened to you that made you so fucked up? I'm curious."

Kenneth, still rubbing the dog's head, said, "Everyone has a cage, either self-created, forced upon them, or some combination of the two. It doesn't matter. I just don't spend as much time as other people contemplating the prospect of release, good or bad."

Cremora said, "It's one thing to be like me, putting up a front. It's another thing to be like you. You don't know the difference any more, do you? You've lost sight."

Kenneth started to say something and then changed his mind. Cremora wanted to ask another question, and then changed her mind. So they sat in the empty lobby of the small-town emergency room, side by side, and said nothing. It was uncomfortable for the first five minutes. After that, the silence itself brought an unexpected comfort to both of them. And the dog from the desert seemed to appreciate it all.

Almost an hour later, the Middle Eastern doctor returned to the lobby.

"Your friend has apparently been bitten by something."

"A spider," Kenneth said.

"Likely," the doctor answered. "He doesn't seem to be suffering an allergic reaction. I don't think the spider or insect was highly poisonous. However, his breast has swollen quite large. I've got some anti-inflammatory samples."

"Can we see his breast?" Kenneth asked.

"That's an odd question, but you can come to the back and see Mr. McAdoo before he's released."

Austin's shirt was off. Kenneth was fixated. "Oh my God," he said upon the sight of Austin's new boob.

Austin said, "Stop, you moron."

"It's not so bad," Kenneth said. "If you just look at the one boob, and nothing else, it's attractive by itself."

He looked at Cremora and asked, "Don't you think?"

Cremora hesitated and then said, "Yeah, I guess so. Does it hurt?"

"Does it hurt?" Austin said. "It hurts like there's a cigarette lighter on my nipple. It hurts like I've been shot, red-hot shrapnel on my nerve ends. Yes, it hurts. I have a very low tolerance for pain anyway."

Cremora asked the doctor, "How long does it take to get from here to Los Angeles?"

"In a car?" he asked.

"Yes."

"Two and a half, three hours. Mr. McAdoo should keep cool and drink lots of fluids."

Kenneth asked, "Can he eat ham, because that's all we've got, ham?"

"Ham is no problem."

"Good," Kenneth said. "Would it be possible for us to get some free samples of painkillers in the event Mr. McAdoo has a problem?"

"I've given him a few, but they're not for you, sir."

"Okay, instead, could you clean my dog's ass with a Q-tip?"

"Oh, Jesus," Austin said.

Kenneth acted confused. "I thought you were a veterinary proctologist. That's what we asked for. We specifically requested a veterinary proctologist."

Kenneth returned to the car first, always conscious of being left behind. Cremora settled in the driver's seat as the nurse helped Austin into the passenger's side.

"Your husband's a lucky man," Kenneth said to the nurse.

"Don't ask him why," Cremora warned.

Kenneth, slightly disappointed, said, "Can you see out of the brown one, or is it just rotten?"

Austin closed the door to create a barrier between the nice nurse and the foul man. He took a deep breath and said softly, "Do you think it might be possible for us to focus on our mission and travel the remaining distance to Los Angeles without speaking a single word? Is that a possibility?"

Cremora started the car.

Kenneth said, "I don't think so. I really don't," and then scratched himself.

CHAPTER 12

Austin felt sleep settle upon him. The pill he was given slowed everything and caused his eyelids to droop. His mind turned home to Emily, and he dreamed of her. She was in the front yard. Austin stood at the window in the dining room, watching her. Emily wore a blue dress, loose and light in the warm breeze. She was barefooted, looking down the neighborhood street, and Austin was struck by her profile, not smiling, but instead, beyond a smile to the edge of satisfaction. A central happiness.

And for no apparent reason, she turned and looked at Austin at the window. Inside of him, Austin felt the butterflies rise in his stomach. There was a distant, unexpected smell of buttery popcorn, and a feeling of utter and complete connection. He was not alone on this planet of six billion strangers, and neither was she, and Austin waited to see her mouth break into a smile, and her barefeet step toward the door of their house. But she didn't move. And the proper amount of time passed by. And Austin came to realize she wasn't coming to the door, but instead, Emily would soon turn and walk away.

The sadness started in the arches of his cyclopean feet and rose like poison smoke through his legs, into his hips, past the once-pink lungs, and invaded his sinuses. In the dream Austin took a long deep breath, slowly filling himself with air, and then just as slowly, releasing the air, trying not to cry. And then she was saying something. Emily's lips were mouthing the words he couldn't possibly hear. So Austin cupped his ear, the universal sign, and Emily raised her voice, but he still couldn't quite capture the words, leaning close to the window, his face contorted.

Emily yelled, "Do you like pie?"

He heard the four words, but certainly, he thought, in a dream such as this, Emily wouldn't have asked, "Do you like pie?"

So she yelled it again, unladylike, "Do you like pie?"

It was unmistakable. The question could not be ignored. So Austin bellowed, both in the dream and from his place in the passenger side of the little red car, "Yes, I like pie."

Kenneth said, "Get the man some pie."

Austin opened his eyes. At first he wasn't sure where he was, but, as he came to his senses, Austin felt the throbbing in his bosom and remembered his circumstances. Kenneth shoved his hand under the driver's seat and pulled out a section of newspaper. On the bottom right corner of the page was a small article. Kenneth read out loud:

"A group of mountain climbers scaling the Alps in Switzerland stumbled upon a curious discovery. As David Chessup approached a high peak on the mountain range, he saw something peculiar. Lined up neatly in the snow were fifty pairs of women's high heeled shoes, side by side, each filled with butter. Chessup said, "We just stood there, all three of us, for a long time, trying to imagine how the shoes got there and why. There were red shoes, white, black, all different colors, facing the same way, all filled with butter. It was a strange thing to see on top of a mountain.""

The car was silent, save for the wind whistling through the busted back window as Cremora, Kenneth, and delirious Austin envisioned the shoes. Cremora wondered if they were all the same size. Kenneth wondered about the butter. Austin was no longer capable of deciding what was a dream and what wasn't.

The radio came to life, the volume as high as it would go, and all three jumped in their seats, some higher than others.

Cremora turned the knob. The man on the radio

said, "Hurricane Austin slammed into the coast of West Florida, just north of Tampa, with winds of 145 miles per hour, a Category Four storm. The tidal surge, combined with the devastating winds and rain, has caused catastrophic damage to this coastal city and surrounding areas. Austin is big, and slow-moving, and angry. A deadly combination. Now back to the hour of power. One hour of average songs that sold over a million copies and captured our hearts."

Kenneth asked, "Is this the end of the freakin' world? I mean, hurricanes, shoes on the mountain, dogs in the desert with doughnuts."

"Doughnuts?" Austin mumbled.

Kenneth zipped past the slip. "I expect to look in the California sky tonight and see the moon on fire. A big ball of sparks and flame. Why not?"

As they drove into Los Angeles, the sun was setting into the Pacific Ocean. The freeway was abuzz, cars whizzing past all round. Cremora hugged the far left lane.

"Where do I turn?" Cremora asked.

Kenneth answered, "Austin's in no condition to walk for miles up and down Hollywood Boulevard. Besides, Emily won't be out there at night. Let's go to the Sunset Strip and mingle with the stars."

Cremora was too freaked out by the traffic to argue, and Austin was still floating in a cloud of spider venom and pain pills. Kenneth barked out instructions until they found themselves on the Strip parked across the street from a trendy Los Angeles bar called *The*

Blue Horse. The sign outside was big and blue, the "H" in Horse flickering like the bulb was going bad when in fact the effect was purposeful, intended to appear rustic and random.

Kenneth said, "I'd like to buy both of you a beer and plate of nachos."

They were hungry and tired and nachos and beer sounded remarkably good.

Cremora asked, "Are we dressed good enough to get in this place?"

"Are you kidding? This is Los Angeles. The rich people dress down. The richer you are, the crappier you look. They'll think we're freakin' millionaires. Oh, but don't let 'em see you get out of this wagon. The rich people might dress crappy, but they don't drive crappy cars."

Kenneth crawled out the window. From sources unknown, Austin experienced a bolt of energy and got out of the vehicle without assistance. Both Cremora and Kenneth felt their eyes drawn to the boob, now the size of a small head of lettuce, pushed against the shirt, creating a one-sided cleavage, which by definition is no cleavage at all, just a juicy mound of flesh. Austin didn't notice the stares. His eyes were busy focusing on the neon blue sign with the flashing "H."

"What kind of establishment is this?" he asked.

"This is where the movie stars and beautiful people sometimes show up to eat nachos. Tonight, we're the beautiful people, believe it or not, so walk like you've been here a hundred times before."

A large Hispanic man with a goat beard and seven earrings in his left ear stood at the door. He eyeballed the three as they came across the street.

Austin whispered under his breath, "He's not going to allow us in. He knows we're not the beautiful people."

As they walked past the large man, Kenneth said, "Hey, Curtis."

The large Hispanic man said, "Hey, Kenny."

Cremora followed Kenneth inside. Austin had noticed the Hispanic man glance down at his chest and quickly back to Austin's face. It was the glance of a man who had seen many things and was surprised by nothing anymore.

The bar was an odd combination of old and new. The wooden bar looked ancient, like something from a cowboy saloon, but all around the walls were strings of tiny blue Christmas lights. A life-size, steel-blue horse with eyes made of crystal stood in one corner, wearing a saddle.

Austin asked, "How do you know that guy?"

"How does anybody know anybody?"

The three sat down at a high table with high chairs. Austin could barely squeeze his backside on the seat.

Kenneth watched and then said, "Have you ever thought about getting that operation fat people get? Sew up your stomach so you can't eat but one cracker at a time?"

Austin responded, "I don't have a problem with my weight and neither does Emily. Unfortunately, they don't have an operation for somebody with your condition."

"Good point," Kenneth conceded. Earlier, he had fished a one hundred dollar bill out of his bag in the car. It was winnings from the roulette wheel. Emily's original thousand dollars was still in the bag, intact, resting in Kenneth's mind with the weight of a hippo.

"Three cold beers and a nacho mountain," Kenneth ordered.

Cremora was intrigued by her surroundings. She held herself out to the world as a person unaffected by glitz and glamour, but inside, she was starstruck just as Emily had always been. As kids, they played for hours and hours pretending to be television stars. Emily was always the pretty one. Cremora was always the smart one who solved the crime, or repaired the jeep, or shot the bad guy in the groin with a bow and arrow.

She scanned the place slowly, stopping on a group of people standing at the bar. There were nine or ten, in their mid-twenties, about half girls. They were loud, and obviously underdressed, and drinking shots of something green. Cremora rubbernecked, stretching to the side to see the faces.

She turned back quickly. "Oh my God."

"What's the matter?" Austin said, but he didn't bother to exert the energy necessary to look over his shoulder at whomever she had seen.

"Oh my God," she repeated. "Do you know who that is over there?"

Kenneth said, "Jimmy Carter?"

"No, you idiot. That's Justin Ross-Blair."

Austin and Kenneth looked at each other. Kenneth said, "I wish it was Jimmy Carter."

Cremora took a look back toward the bar. "Well it's not. It's Justin Ross-Blair."

Kenneth said, "He must be important if he has three names."

With an angry edge, Cremora explained, "He's in the movies. He was just in *Glorious*."

Austin waited for the nacho mountain. He hoped there was sour cream instead of guacamole. The idea of guacamole haunted him.

Kenneth leaned so he could see the crowd at the bar. "He looks like a jackass to me."

"Oh my God. I can't believe he's here. Emily would die."

Austin was curious. He turned his body in the high swiveling chair, lost his center of balance, and fell backwards with such downward speed neither Cremora nor Kenneth moved a muscle. The sound of the great weight and back of the chair crashing to the wooden floor was like an automobile accident. Cremora and Kenneth instinctively got down to help. The group at the bar watched, but in a peculiar way. Almost like it wasn't real. Almost like it happened on a movie screen, far in front, with the hidden knowledge everyone would be okay after the end of the show.

Austin was embarrassed beyond explanation. He scrambled to his feet and looked straight ahead.

"Are you all right, Austin?" Cremora asked. "How many times have I asked you that already today?"

"Nachos," Austin said, as the platter was being delivered. It was a saving diversion. The mound was piled high with chips, meat, tomatoes, and jalapeño peppers. On the top, like a big hat, was a dollop of sour cream the size of a baseball. Bright white and luxurious.

The automobile accident took a backseat to cold beer and the nacho mountain. They ate with greed, each pulling out favorite parts and munching as they searched the mound for more. They didn't notice the beautiful people at the bar snickering. They didn't see the skinny blonde girl do her impression of the nacho eaters, or the handsome movie star pretending he was teetering back on his bar stool.

"Three more cold beers, young lady," Kenneth ordered, and he heard an echo of his order from the direction of the bar, the voice thick with the exaggerated Southern accent only a Yankee could do. But Kenneth didn't react to the insult, and Cremora and Austin didn't hear it.

Finally the mountain was gone.

Austin stood from his chair. "Which way is the boy's room?"

Kenneth took the last swig of his beer. "I've gotta go myself. I'll show you."

The bathroom was fancy. Marble countertops surrounded pure white sinks and gold faucets. Kenneth found a urinal and Austin began to wash his face at the sink. There was no one else in the bathroom. In the mirror, Kenneth saw Justin Ross-Blair come through the door. He swaggered to the sink next to Austin. He was tall, good hair, blue jeans and a funky shirt. He moved like people were watching. "Holy shit. You really busted ass out there, man. That was great," he said in a loud voice.

The two men stood at the sink looking at each other in the big mirror. Justin looked at Austin's breast.

"Is that a tit? You got a giant tit? Are you some kinda circus freak?" He pointed into the mirror instead of directly at the real Austin McAdoo.

Kenneth zipped up and stepped back from the urinal. In a mid-range, commanding voice he said, "Austin, go stand against the door. If anybody tries to come in, put your back into it."

"Who the hell are you?" the movie star said.

Kenneth allowed a minute to pass. He crossed his arms in front of his chest. "Right now, in this bathroom, you might want to ask a different question. You might want to ask, who are these two guys, and what exactly are they capable of doing? Those are more pertinent questions, don't you think?"

Justin cocked his head like a rooster. "Whatever, man."

In a blurry split-second Kenneth rammed Justin Ross-Blair against the bathroom wall. His forearm was hard against the young man's throat. The force and speed left Justin defenseless, face-to-face with what appeared to be a man capable of great violence.

Austin watched from the door. Kenneth, in a soft voice, said, "Being famous doesn't give you a license to be an asshole. You see, in the old days, people were famous for doing things that lifted them above the rest of us, like saving lives, or discovering cures for diseases. Nowadays, fame is heaped upon people for shaking their asses, or accidentally releasing a home porn movie of themselves, or, like you, standing in front of a camera and speaking the lines someone else wrote. Actors are loved because they're unoriginal, and the unoriginal man is loved by the masses. It doesn't mean shit in here. In this bathroom, right now, none of it means anything. I can snap your neck in less than a second and leave you alone on the floor."

The man looked into Kenneth's eyes and knew he spoke the truth. He could only say one word, "Please." And he said it with great meaning.

Austin perspired. He dreaded the idea of the door behind him being pushed from the other side. He'd never been in a true physical altercation, and the idea held much anxiety.

Kenneth whispered, "Now, you can apologize to my friend, or you can listen to the snap of your own neck. You pick."

"It's O.K.," Austin said.

Kenneth turned on Austin, "No, Austin, it's not O.K. If you don't stand up, they'll step all over you. They'll piss in your eye. He's gonna apologize, or I'm gonna kill him, with or without your blessing."

Kenneth eased his forearm from the man's throat to allow enough airflow to speak. "I'm sorry," he said. Mostly he was sorry he found himself in such a predicament, but looking at Austin, the movie star felt a molecule of genuine remorse. He said it again, "I'm sorry."

Kenneth pulled back. He stood five feet away and said, "Now, take off your pants."

"What?" the man said.

"You heard me. Take off your pants."

"Why?"

"Because I'm not interested in you running into the bar to get your buddies or call the cops before we can leave. If you don't have your pants, I bet you won't go out there so fast. I'm sure there's some paparazzo out there just dying to get a picture of Justin Blair-Ross in his underwear, drunk, running out of a public restroom."

"It's Justin Ross-Blair," the young man said.

"See, that's what I'm talkin' about. Take off your pants."

Justin hesitated, "I can't."

"Why not?"

"I'm not wearing any underwear."

"Well, whose fault is that? Certainly not mine. Is that the new thing, no underwear?"

"Pretty much."

"Take off your pants now or I'll slam you against the wall again, crabass."

The young man removed his jeans and stood half

-naked.

Austin and Kenneth watched. Austin was embarrassed and wanted it to end.

Kenneth said, "That's quite an interesting penis you have there. In fact, I'm not sure it actually qualifies as a penis. We need an official ruling."

Justin looked down at himself like it was the first time he'd ever seen it.

"Please don't tell anybody," he said.

"O.K.," Austin answered. "We won't."

Kenneth picked up the pants from the floor. He took another look at the naked man. "I hope you learned something."

Austin led the way out the door taking studder steps, like a trotting horse. Kenneth called the waitress over, but before she could arrive, there was a yell from the direction of the bathroom. "Jason. Jason."

Kenneth looked at Austin. "Bodyguard," he said.

Kenneth put the hundred dollar bill on the table, grabbed Cremora's hand, and they ran like robbers. One of the men from the group at the bar bolted for the bathroom at the same time. "Jason. Jason, get over here," they heard again.

On the way out the door Kenneth said to the doorman, "There's a nude drunk guy in the bathroom with a hacksaw."

Curtis turned and moved quickly inside the bar. Austin and Kenneth, with Cremora in tow, dashed across the street to the red car.

Cremora said, "What's going on?"

"Just drive," Kenneth said.

When down the street, she asked Austin, "What happened?"

"I can't talk about it," he said. A new pressure pounded in his forehead from the exertion of the sprint.

Kenneth spoke up. "Let's go down near Hollywood Boulevard. Unless somebody's got some money, I guess we're sleeping in the car.

They cruised up and down Hollywood Boulevard, half looking for Emily and half looking at the sights. Up on the hill, high above, they saw the Hollywood sign lit up in white lights. It reminded Cremora of her childhood games. It reminded Austin of the half-naked man in *The Blue Horse* bathroom.

Parked on a side street, they settled in for the night.

"Here's the plan," Cremora said, "first thing in the morning, we'll spread out in different directions and agree to meet at the Chinese Theater every hour on the hour. If either of you finds her first, I think I need to do the talking. Agreed?"

It would not be possible for Austin to get comfortable in the small car. He still had a few dollars left for a hotel, but he would need every penny for the wedding expenses. The prospect of confronting Emily the next day was daunting, but the prospect of not finding her was far worse. He hadn't allowed himself to think of the future without Emily. Going back to Birmingham. Unemployed. Living with his mother.

Waking up with the poodle humping the back of his head. It was more than he wished to consider, and now, at this stage of the journey, Austin could barely remember who he once had been.

Cremora started talking, "Why do you need trophies, or money, or even recognition? You've got to be satisfied with the knowledge you're better. The attribute of being smarter dictates that you be satisfied with the knowledge of your superiority alone."

Kenneth opened a canned ham. "Who are you talking to?" he asked.

"Not you," she said, lowering her seat back into a horizontal position. Her head ended up in the backseat area with Kenneth Mint looking down upon her face.

"What is that nasty thing?" Cremora asked.

"My grandmother's hair coat. If you marry me, it's yours."

Sarcastically she said, "Well that's a tempting proposition. What girl wouldn't want a hair coat in return for a lifetime of misery?"

Austin lowered his seat back also, squeezing against Kenneth's leg. It was cramped and warm. Kenneth thought of the hidden thousand dollars and the possibility of getting a hotel room, but he had plans for the money. It was Cremora who had the cash available for the hotel, but she liked the idea of spending the night in a car in Los Angeles under the glowing Hollywood sign on the hill. It was also Cremora who drifted off to sleep first, leaving the two men awake.

Austin touched his boob in the dark and felt the tender pain. He thought of Emily, but his mind swung in another direction and he asked Kenneth, "Would you really have killed that guy?"

"I don't think so. He just pissed me off."

"Do you still have his pants?"

"Yeah. You want 'em?"

"No."

Cremora mumbled something in her sleep about biscuits.

Austin said, "Thanks for sticking up for me, but I could have handled the situation myself. I hope you know that?"

Kenneth chose not to answer. Austin went back to Emily in his mind, closing his eyes and wrapping himself in the blanket of her memory. Tomorrow would be a big day, he thought to himself, one way or another, and he drifted off to sleep to the rhythmic sounds of Kenneth smacking ham.

Part Four

EMILY DOOLEY

"I love to see a girl go out and grab life by the lapels. Life's a bitch. You've got to go out and kick ass." — *Maya Angelou, Poet & Writer*

CHAPTER 13

Kenneth Mint stayed awake all night. He watched people pass on the sidewalk in the dark and listened for sounds. At night, Kenneth felt most like an animal, senses heightened, thoughts clear like the water in a mountain stream trickling downhill. He guessed it was about five o'clock, and very quietly eased his leg from under the tilted front seat to begin the act of crawling out the back window.

Kenneth moved like a sloth. It was important to his plan to leave the others asleep and take his bag of money along. Down the street he turned the corner on his way to Angelo's with the dog from the desert following loyally.

Generally, people are predictable, particularly when they make no effort in the other direction. Emily never considered purposefully becoming unpredictable. It was just her nature, and Kenneth counted on this fact and others in reaching conclusions. He figured she had no idea she was being trailed, was incapable of over-thinking any situation, and loved the idea of getting married. The single most identifiable symbol of marriage is the wedding dress, and Angelo had a shitload of wedding dresses in the window of his shop off Hollywood Boulevard. Besides, Kenneth had noticed Emily jot down the name. If she was still in Los Angeles, he surmised Emily would be drawn to the place like those little yellow goat magnets Kenneth had when he was a kid. Pulled toward each other like gravity askew.

He bought a cup of coffee and sat down in a coffee shop. Out of habit, Kenneth filled the cup to the brim with free sugar and milk. He watched a well-dressed man two tables away pick pieces off a blueberry muffin and shuffle through the newspaper. The man eventually walked away leaving the remnants of the muffin. Kenneth ate most of the remainder, and it was good, soft and pleasant in between sips of coffee the color of new leather. He saved a piece of the muffin for the dog waiting patiently outside. No agreement was reached, no consideration required. Just a bite of warm, soft muffin from man to dog.

There was a wooden bench on the sidewalk a few stores down from Angelo's. Kenneth sat and waited. He thought about dying and how much easier it would be than living. Such thoughts were friendly to Kenneth Mint, much like his boyhood room, warm and familiar. There was no monster under the bed after all, just the future uncertain and all uncertainty holds. He thought of Cremora and tried to dissect the cause of his attraction to her, but recognized the futility before the idea could take root in his mind.

And then Kenneth looked down the street to see Emily Dooley standing at the window of Angelo's dress shop, Glenn resting in her arms. She seemed transfixed on a mannequin wearing an elegant white wedding dress.

Kenneth picked up the dog and walked in her direction. He stopped next to Emily and turned to face the headless mannequin. Emily felt a presence next to her but was unable to turn.

"Hi," Kenneth said.

"Hi," Emily answered.

They stood for a moment. Glenn stretched out to smell the dog. The dog didn't move a muscle, choosing instead to be smelled by the cat and await the cat's decision.

"How did you find me?" she asked, still looking straight ahead.

"Well, my grandmother was full-blooded Orangelo. It was a tribe of people living in the Appalachian mountains until the 1940s. They were much like any other lost tribe of mountain natives except Orangelos have the gift of knowing where people will be at certain moments. I'm one-fourth Orangelo, so I know where people will be one-fourth of the time, often less."

The dog contemplated his options. Flee before the vicious cat pounces, remain motionless and continue to wait, or attack like there's no tomorrow.

"I'm mixed," Kenneth added.

Emily finally turned to look at Kenneth. "I don't believe you."

Kenneth turned his body to face Emily. The dog and cat were now inches apart, but both had decided not to decide.

"O.K., I made that up. But I need to tell you something, Emily, and I need you to listen to me.

"Austin loves you, and I know you love Austin. Yes, you're a weird couple. And, yes, it's hard for the rest of us to understand. But love doesn't know, Emily. Love doesn't know the boundaries or the difference between Austin and Emily or Romeo and Juliet. It just goes where it goes, and it found the two of you, or you found it, or whatever. That's what I've learned from you. We don't have to figure everything out all the time.

"And the stuff in Las Vegas wasn't Austin's fault. It was me. I planned to get your money, get Austin drunk and occupied with the Waffle Hut hooker, and take off with the cash. That was the plan, but for some reason, and I'm still not sure why, I didn't go through with it. Here I am, and here's the money."

Kenneth handed the bag to Emily. The cat took the opportunity to hop down to the sidewalk. The dog looked at Glenn, and then felt himself lowered to the ground and placed next to the wiry gray cat. They were the same height, the dog weighing a few pounds extra, but both held the knowledge that God gave the cat sharp claws. A gift He chose not to bestow upon the dog from the desert. There was a moment of silence, drawn out a moment more, as Kenneth and Emily stood facing each other off Hollywood Boulevard in front of Angelo's.

Kenneth drew a long breath and exhaled slowly. He said, "Don't be like me, Emily."

Emily knew it was a difficult thing for Kenneth to say. She didn't know why, and it didn't matter. She leaned forward, stretched on tip-toes, and kissed the tall man gently on his rough cheek.

"Where is he?" she said with a big smile.

"He'll be at the famous Chinese Theater on the hour. Don't tell him you saw me. Just act like you ran into him by chance. You keep your money, and I'll take the bag. It has my medicine inside. By the way, where's the other cat?"

"He's at the hotel. It's hard to carry two cats. We can get married the day after tomorrow. There's so much to do. A marriage license. A dress. Since Angelo is a friend of yours, can you help us arrange tuxedos for you and Austin? And you need to shave before the ceremony. We can't have a preacher with stubble."

She reached up and touched Kenneth's face with her small hand, turned, and took off down the street in the direction of the Chinese Theater. Emily stopped suddenly, hurried back for Glenn, and took off again. Kenneth looked down at the dog, and the dog looked up at Kenneth. The sun rose impressively in the east, splashing light across the Boulevard.

•

Emily could see Austin's large frame from a block away. She broke into a full sprint. Glenn bouncing in her arms like a sack of new potatoes. Austin was staring down at the handprints of Marilyn Monroe, wondering for a brief moment if her body was buried underneath, like in a mausoleum. He heard the sound of hurry, pivoted in the direction of the sound, and Emily was in his arms like she'd been shot around the world from a cannon.

"You came for me," she yelled. "You love me."

Glenn was smushed between two distinctly different bellies. He squeezed out and landed amongst the stars.

"I'm sorry, Emily. I'm so sorry. I don't like hookers."

"Good," she said, and her feet returned to the solid ground.

Austin swallowed and said what he practiced. "Before I met you, Emily, I always had this lingering feeling that life really wasn't worth the trouble. It was overrated, and sooner or later, one way or another, something would happen to prove the lingering feeling was true. But then I met you."

He couldn't think of the next word. Austin went blank at the exact moment Glenn's needle-like fangs punctured his marshmallow flesh just above the left ankle.

"Ahhhh," and Austin dropped to his knees in pain.

"Emily?" Cremora said.

"Cremora?"

And they hugged. "What are you doing here?" Emily asked, hopping up and down with excitement.

"We came for you. I was in Las Vegas because of the hurricane. I ran into these two idiots and figured they'd never find you without me."

Austin backhanded the cat, sending Glenn spinning into the air like a helicopter blade. Drops of blood soaked into Austin's white socks.

"You can be in the wedding," Emily screamed. "You can be the maid of honor."

Then Emily remembered the fortune cookie. "It's coming true. It's all coming true."

She scurried to Austin, who was still on his knees, the pain finally ebbing. "Remember?" she said. "Remember your fortune? 'A grand and glorious adventure awaits you!' Aren't you glad you ate it? And remember my fortune? 'I will get new shoes.' Look! Look at my feet."

They both looked down to see the shoes Emily had been given by Austin's mother. And then Emily noticed Austin's boob. She looked into his eyes, staring intently, overcome by jealousy and suspicion, triggered by a prehistoric instinct of some sort.

"What's that?" she asked, glancing quickly down and up again.

Austin glanced at his boob, "Oh, I got bit by a spider. It was awful. My nipple's the size of a small frisbee."

Emily digested the explanation and apparently

believed it. "O.K."

Kenneth happened upon the scene. The desert dog was extremely disappointed to spot the cat again. He had hoped the earlier encounter was a one-time thing.

Emily addressed the group. "We've got so much to do. We'll get two rooms at the hotel, one for the boys and one for the girls. Angelo's has the perfect dress, and we can rent tuxedos there, too. And don't forget the marriage license. And the rings."

Emily screamed out, "The rings. Oh my God. The rings.'

On the walk to Angelo's, Austin hung back with Kenneth while the women led the way. He waited until they were a good distance ahead.

"I'm in somewhat of a dilemma," Austin whispered.

"And what dilemma would that be?"

"I hadn't considered the cost of a wedding ring for Emily. It seems to be rather important to her."

Kenneth laughed. "Do you know anything at all about women? If you wanna be around 'em, if you wanna see 'em naked every now and then, you've gotta jump through a lot of hoops, buddy. But I think I can help you with this one."

Kenneth slowed down to allow Emily and Cremora to get even further ahead. He stopped, and then Austin stopped. Kenneth reached deep into his pocket, deeper than it seemed the pocket could go. He fished something out and held it for Austin to see. It was a diamond ring, solitaire, in a gold setting, with six smaller diamonds, three on each side.

Kenneth said, "When my wife walked out I sat around the house feeling sorry for myself. She left her ring on the coffee table. I laid there on the couch and stared at the damn thing. I finally put it in my pocket and left. It's the only thing I took with me, and you can have it."

"Have it?" Austin said.

"Yeah."

Austin suspected foul play. He held the ring up to the sun as if he'd know the difference between a real diamond and a piece of shattered glass. He eyed Kenneth and wondered what else might be in the bottom of that deep pocket.

"Look, it's not stolen. You gave me a ride all the way to Los Angeles. Give the ring to Emily. Bad becomes good. You know what I mean? But I have this idea."

Austin was reluctant to ask. Surely the ring would come with a catch.

Kenneth said, "I think people should enter into marriages for a specific period of time. Say, like three years. At the end of the three years, if one or both of the parties doesn't want to renew the contract, then they go their separate ways. It would just give everybody a light at the end of the tunnel."

Austin said, "You told me that already."

Kenneth felt Cremora's hand pop him upside the head. She'd circled back unnoticed. "What the hell was that for?"

"You gotta ruin everything? They're getting married. There's no contract. There's no three year limit. It's forever. That's what makes it important, turd sack."

Emily came up just in time to hear "turd sack." "What's that mean?" she said.

There was no answer. "What's your dog's name?" Emily asked.

"I don't know his name," Kenneth answered.

"You know what?" Emily said. "We're like the *Wizard of Oz* now. Remember? You're the tin man because you're tall. Austin's the lion because he's big and cute. I'm the scarecrow. Cremora, you can be Dorothy. So the dog is Toto."

Kenneth said, "Toto was gay."

"That's stupid," Emily said. "Toto wasn't gay."

Austin spoke out of turn. "I hated those flying monkeys. It's not suitable for children. Mean monkeys with wings. My mother made me watch it every time it came on television."

Angelo was cross-eyed. It was sometimes difficult to identify to whom he was speaking. His accent was thick Italian.

"Kenny?"

"Angelo."

"I thought you leave California forever?"

"I did. Forever didn't last too long."

"Who you bring with you?"

"Emily and Austin are getting married in two days. She needs a dress, and I guess we need tuxedos, according to the bride."

Angelo turned to face the women. "Oh, you will be a bootiful bride."

"Not me," Cremora said.

"Who?"

"It's not me. I'm not the bride. It's Emily."

"That's who I say."

The women went in one direction, and Angelo stayed with the men to measure for tuxedos. He wrapped the tape around Austin's wide back and stood in front of the monstrous groom. Angelo's eyes were level with Austin's chest. The enlarged tit could not be ignored, but Angelo hesitated to address the subject.

Kenneth stepped in. "It's a tit, Angelo. One big tit. We need to strap it down somehow so it's not so obvious."

Angelo looked up at Austin. "Is it real?"

The question was confusing.

"Is it real?" Austin repeated. He was frustrated by the conversation. "It's flesh, so yes, it's real. It's not a real mammary gland. It doesn't produce milk, if that's what you're asking."

Angelo was perplexed. "I've never seen just one alone without another. Where did it come from?"

Austin grew angry. "Look, Angelo, I need a tuxedo, not a mammogram. I was bitten by a highly poisonous spider. I'm lucky to be alive."

There was a long pause.

Angelo said softly, "Can I see it?"

"Jesus H. Christ, no, you can't see it. What's the matter with you people? You act like I've come into possession of some secret we should all share. Spider. Bit my nipple. Swelled up. Not for you to see. Now can we just get the tuxedo?"

Cremora and Kenneth waited outside while Austin and Emily went inside for their marriage license.

"Haven't you ever wanted to get married?" Kenneth asked.

"Not really. When we were kids, Emily loved everything about weddings. She would dress the dolls and have grand parties. It was like she was born for it."

Kenneth glanced down at her blue jeans and let lust sneak into the conversation.

"What were you born for?" he asked.

She almost caught him looking, but Kenneth was quick.

Cremora said, "Are you asking me if I think I'm gonna change the world? No, I'm not gonna change the world. Are you asking me if there's a point to all this? No, there's no point. There's nothing we can do that makes any difference at all."

She continued, "Isn't that the lesson, how to come to terms with complete futility and still wake up for another day? I think so. You can either drive yourself crazy with it or move along.

"And stop looking at my blue jeans. Lust is so retarded. There are three billion vaginas on the planet. Mine's just as ugly as the rest. You'd be better off dancing alone."

Inside, Austin noted stares from several ladies in the office. Five days a week they watched love bloom in the two red chairs in front of Peggy Panco's desk, but today they saw a 347-pound man with one large breast applying for a marriage license along with a young woman holding a nervous cat.

Emily said to Peggy Panco, "Glenn's gonna be the flower girl. He's not a girl, he's a cat. A boy cat. But still."

"Date of birth," Peggy recited.

"The first time I saw him I knew he was the man for me. The first time. I was buck naked. He was drinkin' a milk punch. I said to myself, 'I'm gonna have his babies'."

Austin smiled proudly and shook his head.

Outside, Kenneth said, "It just seems to me you're bitter before you've had a chance to have your heart broken. Like a preemptive strike, blow all the myths to kingdom come before they can hurt your feelings. What way is that to live?"

"Look, tin man, you're the one without a heart, not me. Everybody's looking for something. The lucky people are looking for something they already have."

Austin didn't realize he'd have to lie in order to receive a marriage license in Los Angeles. On the way walking to the hotel, Emily stopped in a tourist shop. She was surrounded by souvenirs and eventually selected a miniature Grauman's Chinese Theater because the location held special memories.

At the hotel, the dog stood like a statue as Ulysses arched his back and released a long, slow growl. Glenn watched with a smirk. He seemed to have reached the conclusion the dog was harmless and now it seemed humorous for Ulysses to show such fear.

Emily announced, "The wedding is scheduled for 10:00 a.m. sharp, not tomorrow but the next day, on the Julia Roberts star. From now until the ceremony the bride and groom will not see each other. Your room is two floors down. The ceremony will be performed by Kenneth, Cremora will be the Maid of Honor, Glenn and Ulysses will be flower cats, and don't be late."

Later that night, when Kenneth fell asleep in the chair watching a Mexican game show, Austin stretched the telephone cord into the bathroom and sat down to call his mother.

"Mother?"

"No, this isn't your mother. This is Irene, your mother's lesbian lover. I've moved in, killed the poodle, and I'm wearing your favorite underwear on my head."

"Stop it, Mother, this is serious."

"Tell me you found her, Austin. Tell me you found the girl, and you're getting married, and coming home, and planning to spawn."

"We're getting married in two days."

Lila McAdoo stomped her feet on the linoleum kitchen floor and let out a holler.

"Holy crap, there *is* a God. I knew it."

"Settle down, Mother. I need to ask you a question."

Lila changed the channel with the remote. "Shoot."

"Hypothetically, if a wedding ceremony is performed by a person who isn't properly licensed, are the people really married?"

"That's not the question I was looking for, Austin. I thought maybe you would ask something better than that. Don't look for loopholes, boy. It's a wedding. A commitment of the heart. Take the leap without the regrets or don't bother to take the leap at all."

The desert dog let out a single bark at the bathroom door.

Lila asked, "Was that a dog?"

"Yes."

"Did you join the circus?"

"No, Mother, I didn't join the circus. And by the way, why did you always make me watch the *Wizard of Oz* when I was a kid? You knew I was afraid of the flying monkeys."

"It's a good movie. Lots of hidden meanings and important lessons. It ain't about witches and green castles. It's about life, chasing rainbows, figuring out Kansas. The lion found his courage, didn't he?"

Lila lit a cigarette. She switched back to the channel she was watching before. There was a peculiar smell in the house.

"Hey, do me a favor," she said, "during the ceremony, call me on a cell phone and hold it up so I can hear everything. And don't screw this up on purpose, Austin. This is your shot. I've gotta go. My lesbian lover gets jealous when I talk on the phone too long."

She hung up. At first, Austin was angry. As he sat for a moment, the anger drifted away. He was left in the bathroom with a smile on his face.

CHAPTER 14

Austin lay awake in the hotel room for what seemed like hours while Kenneth slept in the chair. The dog found a place at the foot of Kenneth Mint and rested quietly. Austin wondered if Emily, several floors above, was also too nervous to sleep. They would be married in thirty-four hours, less than a day and a half. So much could go wrong. They'd known each other for such a short period of time. Maybe it was all a big mistake, but the train was moving, the date was set, the time had come for change, and sometimes change comes on its own schedule. Even the loudest noises eventually vibrate down to a drone and whisper away in the air.

Austin awoke to the sound of Kenneth in the bathroom urinating with the door wide open. The stream was powerful and lasted an extraordinary period of time. Austin watched Kenneth move to the bathroom mirror, place his right hand on the center of his chest and push slightly. Kenneth struggled to remove the top of a prescription bottle and took a single pill without water to wash it down. He stared at himself in the mirror and then glanced at Austin to notice he was being watched.

"What are you looking at?" Kenneth asked.

"I really think you should wash your hands after you go to the bathroom."

Kenneth examined his face in the mirror. "This is the second conversation we've repeated. It means our relationship is on the decline. I told you already, it's simply not hygienic. Besides, I don't use my hands anyway. I've got a funnel system."

Austin envisioned a series of small funnels, each connected to the one above, attached by metal wires to the underside of Kenneth's private area.

Emily and Cremora were under piles of blankets and pillows in their freezing cold, messy room upstairs. It was like being inside a refrigerator, only with cats. Emily fell asleep early and slept soundly through the night without anxiety or doubt. She snored like a water buffalo.

The night before, she and Cremora made a list on the hotel notepad of everything they needed to accomplish the day before the wedding. The list was long, but neither woman set the alarm clock in the cool, dark room. Cremora loved sleeping more than any other bodily requirement. It was almost a religion for her, with paraphernalia and rituals. She planned a good sleep several days in advance and even owned a sleeping mask made of yak skin.

Emily Dooley dreamed of her life with Austin McAdoo. In the dream, they lived in a tiny apartment in Tokyo and took their meals sitting cross-legged on the floor. She stayed home with the twins and Austin worked as a janitor at a local sports arena. There was a feeling in the dream of serenity. Peaceful color surrounded the Japanese day. Austin accidently dropped the serving spoon in the dream and the sound woke Emily. She smiled and pulled the heavy blanket over the top of her head.

Kenneth said, "Let's go have some breakfast. There's a taco stand down the street."

"My bowels would certainly reject tacos for breakfast," Austin uttered.

"You shouldn't let your bowels make the rules. We're in Los Angeles, Spanish for the City of Angels, and people travel great distances from Mexico to open taco stands here for the purpose of bringing us authentic Mexican treats, like tacos."

Austin sat on the edge of the bed examining the scars left on his ankle by Glenn's fangs.

"That's one of your problems, Kenneth. You don't eat properly."

Kenneth said, "As a matter of fact, last year I was

somewhere in Georgia. I figured out I could go inside the Pancake House, walk around like I was looking for somebody, and fill my pockets with those little packets of Concord grape jelly. When it was crowded, I could pull it off three or four times a day. Maybe get twenty-five or thirty little jelly packets."

Austin had forgotten his anxiety a moment. He looked to Kenneth for the conclusion of the story.

"Only one problem," Kenneth explained, "I started to turn lavender. The natural and artificial coloring in the jelly slowly turned my skin a light shade of purple. People thought I was dying. Hell, I even went to one of those free clinics in the city.

"The doctor said, 'You're not dyin.' You've just gotta stop eatin' so much damn grape jelly'."

The two men looked at each other. Finally Austin said, "Is there a point to this story?"

"There's a point to every story, Austin. Now get up so we can knock down a few tacos."

Emily was in the shower talking about the upcoming honeymoon night. Cremora stood at the bathroom mirror examining herself.

Emily confided, "Austin said he's a loud and boisterous lover. What do you think that means?"

"I'd rather not think about it," Cremora answered.

"I haven't kissed a boy since Ernie Sullivan in high school. He wasn't really a very good kisser. His tongue kept trying to get underneath my tongue, almost like a thumb fight. Mine would be on top, and his would be underneath, and back and forth."

Cremora's skin was pasty. "Sounds very romantic. It makes me want to find Ernie Sullivan and make love to him on a beach."

Steam from the shower drifted over the top of the curtain, colliding with the air from the open door to the bedroom. Emily stopped washing her hair and thought of a question. "Do you ever think maybe you have a twin in this world? An exact twin you never knew you had, out there somewhere, doing things?"

Cremora popped a blackhead. "No."

"And she doesn't know about you, but sometimes you can almost see what she's seeing, or feel what she's feelin'?"

Cremora said, "I bet your twin freaked out when you kissed Ernie Sullivan."

"I'm serious."

"O.K., no, I don't think about a twin. But it's a normal thing. As normal as anything else. You need to hurry up. We've got lots of wedding crap to do."

Emily thought about her dress.

Austin and Kenneth walked down the street together on the way to breakfast.

"Your shirt smells like cat piss," Kenneth said.

"I know," Austin responded. "It won't come out, which is understandable. Cats mark their territory with urine. It was designed to retain its special odor as long as possible in the elements."

They walked along for a while.

"You think you'll ever get used to it?" Kenneth asked.

"I hope not," Austin answered.

They turned a corner, and Austin ran smack into two men. He nearly bowled over the older, smaller man.

When all parties had regained balance, Austin said, "Mr. Lemule?"

Buckshot Lemule said, "Ham thief?"

"What are you doing here?" Austin asked his old boss, the owner of the Dixie Deluxe Canned Ham Company.

"I'm on a business trip. If I wasn't on the way to a meeting, I'd kick your white ass up and down the street. You owe me twenty-two canned hams."

Kenneth was enjoying the situation. "You stole hams?" he asked.

"No," Austin defended. "It was a misunderstanding. Woody must have made a mistake. Besides, you owe me a paycheck."

"I owe you a boot in the butt," the feisty little man said.

Austin ran. It wasn't a conscious choice. He just turned and ran, looking over his shoulder, big arms pumping down Hollywood Boulevard, shoes slapping on shiny stars, the one breast bouncing harder than the other. Gut instinct. Survival. And he ran faster than he'd ever run before, except the time he was chased by the world's largest chicken.

Kenneth hesitated, laughed, and took off after Austin, leaving Buckshot Lemule and the other man standing at the street corner.

The other man said, "He smelled like something bad."

Buckshot watched the two men hauling down the block. Truly, if it weren't for the business meeting, Alvin Lemule would have run the fat man down, tackled him to the cement, and beaten the holy shit out of Austin. It was the way men handled problems. Quick, to the point, and then over. The debt paid with a broken rib, or a chipped front tooth.

Austin ran with the grace and stamina of a wildebeest, finally coming to a stop when his body suggested, standing outside a jewelry store, bent over at the waist, coughing uncontrollably between gasps of polluted air.

Angelo stood next to Emily in her white wedding dress. "You look bootiful," and he smiled.

"There's something wrong underneath my arm. It doesn't fit right."

Angelo patronized the bride. "You just nervous. The dress is fine."

Emily was getting frustrated. "Something's just not right here. See it? Here?"

Angelo waved it off. It was the wrong thing to do. Emily's frustration turned to anger in the time it took for Angelo to circle his nubby Italian hand through the air.

Before Cremora could make it across the room to intervene, Emily had Angelo in a headlock. They fell to the floor together, the bride on top of the olive-skinned dress maker, Angelo's head tight in a vice of white lace.

The man let out a gurgling sound. Cremora got down on her knees and knew better than to try to loosen the grip. Instead, she put her hands on Emily's cheeks, made eye contact, and said, "If you let him up, he'll fix your dress."

Emily froze, slowly loosened the vice, and stood above Angelo as he rolled into a fetal position.

"I'm sorry," Cremora said. "She's just a little on edge about the wedding."

She helped Angelo to his feet. His eyes were still slightly rolled back in his head, and one ear was incredibly red.

"What happened?" he asked.

Cremora seized the opportunity. "You fell."

"I fell?" he asked.

"Yeah, maybe it was something you ate. Rotten sausage or something. You just fell."

Emily didn't like the idea of lying. The poor man's ear looked like a radish.

"I'm so sorry," she said.

Angelo smelled burnt plastic.

Emily said the first thing that came to her mind. "Will you be in our wedding, Angelo?"

Cremora looked at her sideways. Emily stared

back, determined to somehow right her wrong, compensate for nearly squeezing the man's head off his short neck.

"We don't have a best man, do we? Kenneth is doing the ceremony. Angelo can be the best man."

She turned to Angelo. "Please? Could you do it? Cremora won't have anyone to stand with. Pretty please?"

Angelo couldn't remember eating any rotten sausage. His head slowly cleared and the redness turned to pink on the ear.

"Please?" she said, sweetly again.

Angelo, still cross-eyed, looked at Emily, though he appeared to be looking at Cremora, and said, "I will. I will do it."

Kenneth and Austin stood at the window of the taco stand. Two Mexican boys in their early teens were inside, one at the window to take their order, the other behind to prepare the meal. Austin struggled to catch his breath. Beads of sweat the size of corn kernels welled and then rolled down his bloated face.

One of the Mexicans said to his friend, "*Yo pienso que el hombre gordo podr'is morir.*"

Austin asked Kenneth, "What did he say?"

Kenneth answered, "He says you're the size of a sperm whale."

Austin looked with displeasure at Kenneth, who shrugged. He then turned and looked upon the

Mexican boy at the window.

The cook said loud enough to hear, *"Van ellos a comer o no?"*

Austin glanced at Kenneth for an interpretation. Kenneth repeated, "He says he bets you could eat seventy-five bean burritos."

Austin was unsure what to believe. The Mexican kid at the window seemed to have a smirk on his face. Austin tried to take a big breath and began to cough again uncontrollably.

The kid at the window said to his friend, *"Realmente pienso que el gigante podr'is morir."*

Austin regained his breath again.

"What did he say?" he asked.

"He says the giant would taste delicious in a chalupa."

"You're an idiot, Kenneth. I don't believe you speak Spanish. I don't believe you're a preacher. I don't believe you have a license to marry people in California."

It just came out. He'd been wanting to ask, but it just came out, sooner than he'd planned.

Kenneth waited a long moment, turned to the Mexican kid in the window, and said *"Yo tendre' tres tacos, con todo, y un Coque. El gigante tendra' una mierda burrito y un vaso de la orina de burro."*

The Mexican kid turned around to his friend and barked out the order in English, "Three tacos, with everything, Coke, and the Giant wants a shit burrito and a glass of donkey piss."

Austin listened to the order. He finally said, "I'm not eatin'."

"Why not?" Kenneth asked.

Emily, Cremora, and the wedding dress left Angelo's shop. It was a beautiful day and Emily hoped the next day would be equally beautiful. She was satisfied with her apology to Angelo and also satisfied with the dress after alterations to the armpit area.

From behind she heard, "Vanessa?"

The name didn't ring any bells, and she walked along, almost skipping, down Hollywood Boulevard.

"Vanessa?" she heard again.

Emily had almost forgotten her stage name. Even though it was only days away, it seemed like years. She turned around to see Alvin Lemule.

"Buckshot?"

"What are you doin' here, girl?"

Emily hugged him like she'd hug an uncle. Cremora and the younger man stood by and waited, nodding the way people do in such situations.

"Oh, my God," Emily said. "What are you doing in California?"

"I'm out here on business. What are you doing here?"

Emily said, "I'm getting married, tomorrow, here, on Julia Roberts' star."

She noticed Cremora. "Oh, this is Buckshot. He was one of my best customers, and nicest, back in

Tampa."

She turned to Buckshot. "Remember the time you gave me two hundred dollars to put your eye next to my nipple as close as you could without touching?"

Alvin Lemule smiled. The man with him seemed confused.

"Anyway," Emily said, "can you come to the wedding? Please? Please? It's tomorrow, at ten o'clock in the morning, on Julia Roberts' star. You can meet my husband."

Buckshot Lemule had lusted for many women in his life, but few like he lusted for Vanessa. He found reasons to travel to Tampa, frivolous reasons, untrue reasons, and left his wife behind for short so-called business trips. But Buckshot was a realist. He knew his time with Vanessa was short, and she would move along, and he'd find another stripper in another dance club willing to sit with him naked while he sipped whiskey sours. He also remembered looking at her nipple a quarter inch from his eye.

"Yeah, I'll come," he said.

Emily smiled. She leaned over and gave the crusty man a kiss on the cheek.

"Oh yeah," she said, "my name's not Vanessa. It's Emily." And then she turned and walked away.

The other man waited a few moments and said, "You sure know a lot of people, Mr. Lemule."

"Well, Corey, I don't believe in coincidences. This happened for a reason. Remember that."

•

After leaving the taco stand, Kenneth and Austin went to Angelo's to pick up the tuxedos. Austin's enlarged breast had reduced in size but still stood out prominently.

Angelo seemed disoriented. First he brought out two very small brown tuxedos from the back room.

"I don't believe these'll fit, Angelo. Why's your ear red?"

Angelo touched his ear the way a man might touch the ear of a baby.

"I fell," he said.

"When?" Kenneth asked.

"Today."

"Where?"

Angelo pointed to the floor where earlier he'd rolled into a protective fetal position.

"Why'd you fall?" Kenneth asked.

Angelo mumbled something about sausage and went away to the back room.

Austin said, "I don't like your friend Angelo very much."

"Why not?" Kenneth asked.

Angelo reappeared with the correct two tuxedos. Austin's shirt had been specially altered to accommodate his larger tit.

"How much do we owe you?" Kenneth asked.

"Half-price rental," Angelo said. "I look forward to standing at your wedding, Mr. Austin. In my country it is great honor to be best man."

Austin looked at Kenneth, and Kenneth shrugged his shoulders.

"Half price is half price," Kenneth said.

Angelo went again to the back room.

Austin whispered, "I don't want him to be my best man. I don't even like him. I can't tell who he's talking to."

"Maybe you can get to like him after the wedding. Like he's a future best man. A best man to be."

Angelo returned holding his tuxedo, a match to the others.

"I will see you tomorrow," he said. "Now I go lie down."

Austin and Kenneth stepped outside into the clear day.

"I'm going to the room and taking a hot bath," Austin announced. "So far today I've encountered my nemesis, Alvin Lemule, on the street corner, been mocked by two Mexican tacomakers, and presented with the knowledge that the best man at my wedding will be a smelly little cross-eyed man I neither like nor wish to be near."

"Maybe I could score us a little weed," Kenneth said.

Austin and Kenneth looked at each other for an extended period, neither willing to move, both trying to gain a bit of insight into the other as a reaction to the weed comment. It could go either way. There was internal teetering, mental trench warfare, deteriorating into a staring contest.

Finally, Austin broke away and walked to his room imagining hot bath water and maybe, just maybe, volumes of white bubbles.

Emily stood in the hotel bathroom looking at herself in the mirror once again. The wedding dress seemed even brighter white in the fluorescent lights. Cremora lay on the bed next to Ulysses. His long orange body stretched as far as possible, and then he rolled onto his back, belly to the ceiling. The room was a royal mess. Clothes and towels were strewn around like a tornado had touched down for a brief second and quickly bounced away. Glenn enjoyed rooting into obscure piles and leaving a few magic drops of tinkle. In fact, he lived for it.

Cremora usually thought first before speaking, but sometimes, if she was in a very comfortable situation, she would say things as they popped into her mind without a filter.

"What do you think of Kenneth?" she said aloud.

Emily stopped adjusting her veil and leaned slowly through the bathroom doorway to look at Cremora. Cremora saw her look.

"What?" she asked.

Emily smiled. "You gotta little crush on Kenneth?" she whispered like it was a secret.

"No," Cremora countered. "He's a freak. Besides, I don't have crushes."

Emily leaned back to her spot in front of the

mirror. She said, "Sometimes we don't get to choose."

"Wrong," Cremora explained. "We always choose. Life is about the choices we make and the choices we don't. It would be nice to believe they're made for us, certainly would remove the everyday pressure, but it all comes down to me, ultimately."

Emily knew better. She'd seen fate collide with her own two eyes, and once you've seen it, there's no going back.

Emily leaned through the doorway. She and Cremora locked eyes. Emily smiled a knowing smile. Cremora waited for her to go back to adjusting the veil, and then Cremora found herself smiling also.

Austin lay awake the night before his wedding. It was 2 a.m., and he wasn't tired in the slightest. Twice he'd gotten up to call his mother, and twice Austin had resisted the temptation and crawled back in bed.

Kenneth was asleep in the chair in front of the television. The same Mexican game show flashed across the screen with the sound very low. Kenneth's dog slept soundly at his feet. The hotel accommodations had not been part of the doughnut bargain, but the dog was obviously pleased with the arrangement.

Austin entertained the thought of packing his bags quietly, sneaking to his red car, and driving away from California. He took the plan in his mind from beginning to end, working through every detail, and then decided not to move from his place in the comfortable bed. He dissected the reasons for his inaction. Fear. Laziness. Or maybe it was just the wrong thing to do. He loved Emily more than anything he'd ever loved in this world. More than he imagined possible the night he set foot in the establishment in Tampa, Florida and balanced on the barstool in front of a cool milk punch. More than his mother had loved his father, or Caesar had loved Cleopatra, or anybody loved anybody, ever, in the history of civilization. And so he didn't get out of bed and pack his bags, or sneak out to the car, or drive away from California. Instead, Austin McAdoo steadied himself for the ultimate commitment, a promise to love for all eternity, with the fall-back position that the preacher might not be properly licensed to perform a lawful marriage.

CHAPTER 15

Emily looked out the window at the new morning.
The sky was blue. It was the day she'd waited for her
entire life. The culmination of so many wishes. She
shook Cremora until there was a moan underneath
the blanket. Emily wanted to get down to the street
in plenty of time to locate the Julia Roberts star and
watch the other people arrive.

Austin slept a total of thirty minutes before the sunlight
from the window caused the insides of his eyelids to
turn a creamy shade of orange. He took a deep breath
and moved his hands to the enlarged breast. There
was still a soreness inside, and the boob filled Austin's
huge hand. He touched the nipple tenderly and then
withdrew his hand, feeling self-conscious.

From across the room, Kenneth said, "Are you

touching yourself?"

Austin sat up. "No."

Kenneth said, "I think you touched yourself, thinking about the honeymoon tonight."

"You're a moron," Austin responded.

"Maybe," Kenneth said, "but you got caught touching yourself, not me. It's time to put on the monkey suits. We've got to find this Julia Roberts star. Who is Julia Roberts anyway?"

"I'm not sure," Austin said. "I think she's in the movies."

The two men stood in front of the mirror shaving. Kenneth dry-shaved with no cream, scraping across his face. Austin lathered up excessively, carefully negotiating the area under his nose as if the skin was made of paper.

"You've got a clump of fur on the back of your neck," Kenneth said.

Austin glanced at Kenneth in the mirror and tried to turn his body to see the clump. He was able to spot a portion of the neck hair, black and unattractive. Austin tried to bend his thick arms to reach the spot but couldn't quite get there.

Kenneth shook his head. "Stay still," he said, moving behind Austin to take care of the problem.

Kenneth shaved Austin's neck area with the same lack of caution he shaved himself. The coarse black hairs gathered on the razor until the blade struck something meaty.

"Ahhh," Austin bellowed.

"What?" Kenneth asked.

But then Kenneth could see the blood. He'd shaved off a large brown mole, the top hanging loose, blood pouring from the hole like a breach in the dam.

Austin turned on Kenneth, "What have you done? You tried to decapitate me. Lord God Almighty."

"Shut up," Kenneth said. "It's just a mole. I did you a favor. Who the hell wants a mole on their neck?"

It took ten minutes to stop the bleeding. The bathroom looked like a M.A.S.H. unit, but eventually the two men stood in front of the bathroom mirror together in their tuxedos.

"You can barely see the tit," Kenneth said.

Austin turned his body for a profile view. Kenneth was right. He could barely tell one breast was significantly larger than the other.

"I'm not wearing this tuxedo jacket," Kenneth said. "Instead, in honor of my grandmother, I'm wearing the hair coat."

Austin watched Kenneth remove the tuxedo jacket and put on the coat of human hair. He decided not to have a conversation about the coat. There were other things to worry about.

"Do you have the ring?" Kenneth asked.

Austin checked his pocket for the eleventh time. He felt the small bulge of the gold ring. For something so tiny, it seemed enormously important. Austin checked for the twelfth time and then once more on the way out the door.

•

Glenn and Ulysses wore special collars for the occasion. As flower cats their role was undefined, yet somehow critical to the entire proceeding. Emily, in full wedding dress, carried Glenn down Hollywood Boulevard. She let Cremora tote Ulysses because she decided Ulysses was less apprehensive about the upcoming ceremony and therefore less likely to cause a scene.

Emily stopped at the first tourist map salesman. "Can you tell us where Julia Roberts' star is?"

The older Hispanic man seemed instantly baffled by the question. "Who?"

"Julia Roberts. The movie star."

The man pulled out and opened a large map of the Hollywood Walk of Fame. He scanned the names with his finger. Emily watched him, amazed that any professional Walk of Fame map salesman wouldn't know the exact location of all 2,156 stars.

"Julia Roberts," she repeated sternly.

The man casually said in broken English, "Today is my first day. I don't see any Julia Roberts."

"Are you stupid?" she asked.

The man didn't answer. He finally said, "You want to buy a map?"

Emily set off, map in hand, wishing she'd listened to Austin that day in the car when he tried to explain map reading. It looked like a random piece of modern art to her, roads and numbers, special colors, with an index on the back listing all the names.

They walked quickly. "Let me look at the map,"

Cremora said from behind, but Emily just went from one star to the next, looking at the names below her feet. They were names she didn't recognize. People she'd never heard of. Emily stopped and waited for Cremora to catch up.

"Is there another Walk of Fame?" Emily asked.

Out of breath, Cremora answered, "No, Honey. Slow down. This is the only Walk of Fame."

Cremora scanned the names in the index.

Emily said, "Maybe her star is under her maiden name."

"Maybe she doesn't have a star," Cremora said.

Emily gritted her teeth and looked down. "If they'll give a star to Pee Wee King, they better give a star to Julia. That's all I have to say," and she turned and began walking again, looking down at each star she passed.

As they stepped out on the street, Kenneth said, "What time is it?"

"I don't know," Austin answered.

"Why do you wear that idiotic watch if it doesn't work?"

"As a protest to international timekeeping methods."

"Oh," Kenneth said. "What a rebel."

They arrived at the same tourist map salesman. Kenneth said to the older Hispanic man, "Where is the Julia Roberts star?"

The man looked dumbfounded. "I don't know,"

he said.

"You don't know?" Kenneth responded. "Maybe you need to find another job."

The man said to Kenneth, "What kind of coat is that?"

"A human hair coat, my man. Woven from my grandmother's hair."

The man made a face of disbelief and then touched the coat gently between his index finger and thumb. He shook his head up and down, apparently satisfied with what he felt.

Austin bought a map, and they began to roam the square blocks comprising the Hollywood Walk of Fame. As Austin walked, his shirt collar moved up and down, irritating the place the mole used to be. The spot began to bleed, and the blood soaked slowly into the white collar, causing a small bright red stain.

As they walked and walked, the heat of the day got underneath their clothes and sweat started to eke out. Kenneth asked the man on the street the time of day.

"Nine forty-two."

"Oh, Lord," Austin mumbled. "I can't find Julia Roberts on the list. This is a bad sign. This is a bad omen. We're supposed to get married in eighteen minutes. Where is Emily?"

"Don't panic," Kenneth said. "I had no idea there were this many famous Pee Wees in the world. Pee Wee Hunt. Pee Wee Herman. I saw a Pee Wee King. Why would anybody let themselves be called Pee Wee?"

Austin stared at Kenneth as he spoke. Kenneth

noticed the blood on Austin's collar but stopped himself from saying anything. After all, it was Kenneth who sheered off the brown mole and started the flow of blood. There was no sense alarming Austin, he thought. The big man was already alarmed enough.

Emily was in a total frenzy. The cats were restless. No one they asked could remember where the Julia Roberts star was located. Emily had no idea there were so many stars spread over so many blocks. She felt the sweat under her wedding dress and blisters began to rise where her shoes rubbed. It was nine fifty-nine, one minute before she was to be married.

Emily suddenly turned around. She saw the enormous frame of a tuxedoed man halfway down the block, emerging from behind a small crowd of tourists. At the exact moment, Austin spotted the outline of a white wedding dress up ahead.

"There he is," Emily whispered to Cremora.

"There she is," Austin said aloud to Kenneth.

And they began to move toward each other. The space between them lessened with every step, with the passing of any star, and Emily smiled her beautiful smile, and Austin felt a feeling come to his body like he was walking on water.

Fifty yards. Twenty. Ten. And then Austin took Emily in his arms and held her like his life dangled by a thread, and Emily began to cry. She looked down to see they were standing on the star of Ann B. Davis.

"This is where we will be married," Emily said.

"What about Julia Roberts?" Austin asked.

"Right here," Emily said, "where God has brought us together. Right here on the star of Ann B. Davis."

"Who is Ann B. Davis?" Austin asked.

"The maid from *The Brady Bunch*."

Austin hesitated, but only slightly. "O.K."

"Why did you have to wear that coat?" Cremora asked Kenneth.

Kenneth looked down at the coat. "Let the ceremony begin," he announced.

"Hold on," Austin said. "Cremora, could you call my mother on your cell phone? She wants to hear the wedding."

The number was dialed and the phone began to ring.

"Hello."

"Mom?"

"Don't tell me any crap about the wedding being cancelled," she said.

"No, it's not cancelled. I'm gonna let Cremora hold the phone for you to hear."

Angelo happened upon the scene dressed in his matching tuxedo. "I cannot find a Julia Roberts star."

"Who was that?" Austin's mother asked.

"Angelo," Austin said.

"Who the hell is Angelo?" Lila McAdoo asked.

"My best man," Austin said reluctantly.

"Never heard of him," Lila said.

"Just be quiet, Mother. Kenneth is going to start

the ceremony."

"Kenneth who?"

"Kenneth Mint."

"Little Kenny Mint? The kid from your school? He's a shithead."

Austin gave the phone to Cremora who held it up while she grasped Ulysses in the other. Before Kenneth could begin, Buckshot Lemule was suddenly standing next to Emily.

"Hey, girl," he said.

"Oh, you made it. Thank you," Emily said.

Buckshot looked at Austin and asked, "What is this jackass doing here?"

"This is Austin McAdoo, my fiance."

Alvin Lemule squinted his eyes and held his tongue for the sake of Vanessa.

"How do you know him?" Austin said, pointing at Buckshot Lemule.

Before anyone could answer, Kenneth said, "Can we get this show on the road? This coat is hot as hell."

In the phone they could hear the sound of a barking white poodle.

"Shut your trap, Lafitte," Lila McAdoo said through the phone loud enough to be heard by everyone at the ceremony.

Austin rolled his eyes. Angelo saw the blood on the white collar, now twice the size as before.

"You bleeding on my shirt," Angelo yelled.

Austin put his hand to the spot and felt the warm blood pouring from the cut. He suddenly felt dizzy and swayed noticeably. Angelo positioned himself on one side of the groom, Buckshot Lemule on the other. Austin found himself supported by two small men he never imagined appearing on his special wedding day.

Kenneth began, "The greatest misconception is the belief we must fully understand anything of true importance in this life, especially love.

"That having been said, God has decided to cast his spell on Austin McAdoo and Emily Dooley, empowering and crippling them at the same time with the wonder of love. A love for one another so strong, so enduring, it surely will last beyond this life and into the next."

A few people on the street stopped and watched the proceeding. Glenn released one of his patented howls, but the sound brought no response. Lila McAdoo, standing in her kitchen in Birmingham, felt her eyes well up for the first time in many years. She took a short drag of her cigarette and pushed the phone harder against her ear so she wouldn't miss a word.

Austin began to feel his legs again. Emily's smile was remarkable.

"Austin?" Kenneth said. "Do you take Emily Dooley to be your lawfully wedded wife? Do you promise to love her even when you might not like her, lust for her when she becomes old and saggy, and cherish her as your best friend, companion, and wife for all eternity?"

Austin looked at Emily in her white dress holding

Glenn.

"I do," he said, and he meant it.

Cremora felt a weakness just behind her knees, and a lump in her throat. A few more people gathered, and they all stood in a semi-circle in the sunlight on Hollywood Boulevard.

"Emily?" Kenneth said.

"Yes."

"Do you take Austin McAdoo, the giant pilgrim, to be your lawfully wedded husband? Do you promise to take care of him when he drives you nuts, respect him no matter what the day brings, and provide him lots of physical love when you don't feel like it?"

Kenneth winked openly at Austin.

"Also Emily," Kenneth said, "do you promise with all your heart to love Austin for eternity, so help you God?"

Emily looked up at Austin, the blood trickling in a small line down the edge of his collar.

"I do," she said, and she meant it.

"Thank you, Jesus," Lila McAdoo offered through the phone.

"The ring please," Kenneth said.

Austin felt for the familiar bulge in his pocket. He pulled out the diamond ring, held Emily's free hand, and slipped the ring on her finger.

Emily was mesmerized. She held the ring to her face and stared at the diamond. She pulled it off her finger and examined the prize. Inside was an inscription. Emily held it up and focused on the tiny words. Out loud she read, "You're a fine piece of ass."

Austin looked at Kenneth in horror. Kenneth had forgotten the long-ago love-induced inscription. His eyes widened in surprise. Austin swallowed hard. He turned back to Emily, expecting the very worst, prepared to explain everything.

Emily looked up at Austin. The smile widened across her face. She nearly screamed where she stood, bursting with pride and happiness.

"I love you, Austin," she said.

Kenneth jumped in, "With the powers vested in me by the great state of California and/or God, I now pronounce...."

The words stopped abruptly. Kenneth felt a catch in his chest. His breath stopped short. A thin line of pain traveled from the center of his torso up the shoulder and down into the arm. Agony formed slowly across Kenneth's face.

"Are you O.K.?" Angelo asked.

Kenneth forced himself to speak, "I now pronounce you man and wife."

Kenneth Mint dropped hard to his knees. At first, Cremora thought it was part of Kenneth's crazy show, maybe the beginning of a prayer or a sacrament to the hair coat. But then she saw Kenneth's face, and his hand rising up to clutch his heart.

Buckshot Lemule rushed forward with Cremora. Ulysses went flying. They reached Kenneth before he fell forward onto his face and helped him gently down upon the star of Ann B. Davis. They rolled Kenneth on his back. Cremora hung up on Lila McAdoo and called for help. When the phone went dead, Lila threw it across the kitchen in celebration of her son getting married to a beautiful, simple girl named Emily Dooley in Los Angeles, California, on a warm blue morning. A few minutes later she lit another cigarette and began to decorate the spare bedroom for her future grandchildren, Emma and Pierre.

CHAPTER 16

Cremora Watson sat by Kenneth's bedside at the hospital. She still wore the maid of honor dress. Austin, Emily, Angelo, and Buckshot Lemule waited in the lobby. When the nurse had asked her name, Cremora lied and said, "Cremora Mint, Kenneth's wife." Under the circumstances, not many questions were asked and she found herself at Kenneth's bedside.

The doctor said, "It looks like he had a heart attack. Any history of heart trouble?"

Kenneth was drifting at the edge of consciousness. Cremora looked at him for an answer to the question. Kenneth shook his head, yes.

"Prior heart attack?" the doctor asked.

Kenneth shook yes again.

"Any medication?"

Cremora handed the doctor the empty pill bottle the nurse had removed from Kenneth's pocket.

In the silence between questions came the shrill sound of the butt whistle. The doctor looked up from his chart. Cremora stared at the floor like she'd heard nothing. Kenneth smiled slightly to himself and then drifted into a dream. He was on a boat, a white sailboat, with the ocean breeze in his face. There was a woman down below in the cabin. In the dream, Kenneth couldn't see her, but he knew she was there, doing something in the tiny kitchen, and soon she would come out and join him topside. Her presence held its own feeling.

In the lobby, Angelo insisted Austin remove his shirt to begin the process of dissolving the bloodstains as soon as humanly possible.

"If you refuse to give the shirt, I must charge you full price," Angelo barked, standing a safe distance from Emily.

Austin was tired of fighting with the little man. Unfortunately, in the craziness, Austin had forgotten his enlarged breast. As he removed the shirt in the open lobby, Alvin Lemule got a glimpse of the man-tit.

"What in God's name is that?" he said.

Austin covered his bare nipple with the jacket.

"Nothing," he said.

"Nothing, my ass. Emily, the man's got a boob. I saw it."

"I was bitten by a highly poisonous spider. It nearly killed me," Austin explained.

Emily touched Austin's arm. She was shaken by Kenneth's heart attack, and the wedding, and concerned about the impending honeymoon discomfort. Buckshot sensed Emily's fears and quickly misinterpreted the problem.

"Look," Buckshot said, "maybe I pulled the trigger too fast when I fired you, McAdoo. How about this? My wedding present to you, to both of you, is Austin's job back. After the honeymoon, come see me. I think we can work something out."

"Thank you," Emily said, though she hadn't had a thought about how they planned to support themselves when the money ran out, and there wasn't much left.

Cremora appeared in the lobby. The others turned to her for news.

"The doctor says Kenneth will be all right. He's got to stay a few days for some tests. I'll stay here with him tonight. Emily, you and Austin enjoy your last night in the hotel. I'll come by in the morning. Here's the key to our room."

Austin reluctantly took the key. Angelo turned and walked away without a word, confident he could remove the blood stain from the shirt collar and seemingly uninterested in whether Kenneth would live or die.

Buckshot Lemule shook hands with Austin and gave Emily an inappropriate kiss goodbye, putting his lips to hers and pressing a bit too hard. Cremora went to Kenneth's room, and Austin and Emily started walking back to the hotel, Emily in her wedding dress, Austin shirtless with a tuxedo jacket barely covering his chest.

"Do you want your old job back?" Emily asked.

"I hadn't really thought about it."

"It was nice of him to offer," Emily said.

"I suppose so, but if you'll recall, I wasn't fired. I submitted my resignation."

"I guess so," Emily said.

They walked down the street in no hurry. It was hot, but both were filled with thoughts and fears about the night ahead.

"I've never had sex before," Emily said softly.

Austin was relieved and horrified at the same time.

"Neither have I," he said.

Emily smiled. "You're lying."

"No, I'm not. I swear."

They walked along further, both thinking. Finally Emily said, "How are we gonna know what to do?"

Austin thought a moment and answered, "How did Adam and Eve know what to do?"

Emily hadn't thought of that. "You're right. They didn't have books back then, or movies. They must've figured it out by themselves."

"I guess so," Austin said.

"So can we," Emily added.

And they did. Over a period of twelve hours they figured it out at least six times. They laughed, and looked around on each other, and sprinted naked from the bed to the bathroom, and touched, and felt things they'd never felt before. They stayed awake all night, and ordered room service twice. Glenn cowered in the corner under a chair. Austin was quite sure there were no names for some of the positions they tried.

In the morning, Emily stood in front of the bathroom mirror, holding up her ring hand. She whispered, "Mrs. Emily McAdoo, you're a fine piece of ass," and Austin heard her and couldn't help but smile to himself.

There was a knock on the door. Emily answered, wearing only a towel, and Austin pulled the covers up to his third chin. Cremora walked inside the room.

"Did I interrupt anything?" Cremora said.

"We were just starting to pack. Check-out time is only an hour away," Emily said. "Can you be ready to leave by then?"

Cremora began to sort through the piles of clothes and shove items in her backpack.

"I'm not going," she said.

"What?" Emily asked.

Cremora explained, "I've decided to stay here, in Los Angeles, with Kenneth for a while. He needs me, and besides, I don't want to go back. There's nothing in Tampa for me, even if old Hurricane Austin spared us too much damage. You can have everything in the apartment if you want."

Austin, remembering the words of a conversation from earlier days, said, "Who gets the frozen cat turd?"

Cremora smiled. "You can have that, Andre. Consider it a wedding present."

Emily said, "You and Kenneth will make nice babies. You both have red hair."

Cremora pretended to ignore the comment. "Austin, I've got the key to your room. I'm gonna get Kenneth's stuff and the dog. We'll keep the dog."

"Oh, please don't," Austin mocked. "I so love the dog from the desert. I would like to breed him and sell his priceless pups."

And then Cremora was gone. The train was on the move again. Change was coming. She walked down the Los Angeles street with only a bag full of clothes, a dog with no name, and the brilliant unexpected thought of beautiful red-headed girls playing in the yard while she and Kenneth watched from the porch swing.

It took a while to get everything situated in the little red car. Austin was pleased when it started on the first turn of the key. The trunk was packed tight with suitcases and all the remaining hams. Glenn and Ulysses had the backseat all to themselves, and the busted rear window promised airflow in place of air conditioning.

Emily shoved a toothpick into the window button and miraculously the electric windows came to life. She reached her hand around the back of the radio, yanked a few wires, and suddenly there was music.

Sitting in the car, ready to go home, Austin unveiled his new road map. He had outlined in bold red marker the route home, purposefully avoiding the location of the death of the world's largest chicken. Emily had a new respect for maps. She listened while Austin authoritatively explained each anticipated twist and turn on the road from Los Angeles to Birmingham. Austin even had gas station stops marked in different color ink.

As he started to pull out from the parking spot onto the road, Austin saw a white envelope at his feet. He tried to reach it, pulled back, and tried again, still not able to touch the edge. Emily nimbly squeezed through and pulled the envelope from behind the accelerator.

It was the envelope they found on the grave of Austin's father in Las Vegas, New Mexico. Austin veered out in the traffic. He remembered the words inside the envelope, "Don't make the same mistakes I made." Without much thought he tossed the envelope out the open window onto Hollywood Boulevard to be swept away by the hot wind.

"Don't worry, Lovin' Mustard Man," Austin said out loud.

As the car slowly passed the taco stand, one of the Mexican boys spotted Austin. He nudged the cook and pointed. The first Mexican boy yelled, "*El Gigante! El Gigante!*" and waved.

Austin, like a man in his own parade, stuck his hand out the window and acknowledged the crowd with a few turns of the wrist. Emily, for unknown reasons, was impressed by this display. She looked over at Austin like he was some sort of celebrity, which, as a matter of fact, he was, even if he would never be formally acknowledged with a star on the Hollywood Walk of Fame.

As they rose up onto the highway, heading east into the heart of America, Emily McAdoo, her eyes straight ahead, gently slipped her tiny hand into the hand of Austin McAdoo as it rested on his broad thigh. They stayed that way a long time. It was a perfect fit.

Acknowledgments

I need to thank my wife, Allison, Dusty, Mary Grace, Lilly, and Marlin. My father and Virginia, my mother and Skip, Sally, Bob & Ellen, Bill & Linda, Sharon Hoiles, Big Daddy, Russ, Joy Larson for the shoe thing, Linda Vernon, Angie Kaiser, Cindy Jackson for the Spanish interpretation, Joel Stabler, Smokey Davis, Sweet Sonny Brewer, Barry Munday, Shauna Mosley, Rich Green, Robert Bell, and of course David Poindexter, Kate, Danny, Dorothy, and the spirit of MacAdam/Cage.

About the Author

Frank Turner Hollon lives in Alabama with his wife and children. He is the author of *The God File*, *A Thin Difference*, *The Point Of Fracture*, *The Wait*, and *Life Is A Strange Place*, which was developed into the movie Barry Munday. Frank is currently assisting with the screenplay for his novel *blood & circumstance*, scheduled to begin filming this year, and finishing his latest novel *The Book of Neil*, which will be published in the fall of 2012.